AFTER
Eve

JB LEXINGTON

———

HADLEIGH HOUSE
PUBLISHING

Hadleigh House Publishing
Minneapolis, MN
www.hadleighhouse.com

Cover art by Gee Gee Collins.
ISBN-13: 978-1-7326347-9-4
ISBN-13: 978-1-7357738-0-3 (ebook)
LCCN: 2020919922

HADLEIGH HOUSE
PUBLISHING

To my loves . . . D-J-B

AFTER

Eve

1

The horizon is pregnant with the setting sun, and the view from my vantage point is where I'm meant to be forever. A soft, rhythmic beat from his pulse penetrates my heart so deeply I can't stop the small tear that escapes the crease of my eye. It rolls across my cheek onto his neck.

He reaches down and tilts my head up and regards me with concerned eyes. "What's wrong, my love? Don't stain that beautiful postcoital glow with unnecessary tears."

"Oh nothing," I sniffle.

"Jones, I know you."

Our lips meet again, and this time with passion. I roll on top of him, and I feel his readiness between my legs.

"Jesus! Jones, you are going to give me a heart attack," he says, panting. "I'm not as young as I used to be."

"You're just going to have to learn to keep up with me, old man." I giggle and pull at the little gray hairs on his chest. Our seventh round of lovemaking is interrupted by the sound of my cell phone. I whine into our kiss.

"I'm sorry, baby. I have to get it. I'm on call." I kiss his nose and dismount my straddle.

"Dr. Jones speaking." I look over at Henry's Adonis body, lying and waiting on the bed. He's stroking his beautiful cock to maintain what I started. I have to look away. It's just too distracting. We've been married for five years, and I still can't get enough of him.

"Okay, Mr. Smith, call my office and speak with Dottie, and she'll book you in for Monday. No, I'd advise against going to see your wife at her workplace to clear the air. That's definitely not a common-ground space to discuss marital issues. No, no, yes, that's correct. Like I said, call Dottie, and tell her I said you can book the first two hours of my day. No, that's okay. You haven't ruined my weekend. Don't worry—yes, I'll see you Monday." I hang up and toss my phone onto the pink velvet chair in the corner and saunter back to my gorgeous husband and slide slowly back onto him.

"Now, where were we?" I moan.

Henry tilts his head back with appreciation and inhales through clenched teeth. The sound of my cell interrupts us again. We look at each other, worry reflected in our eyes. It's the ringtone I have designated for my mother.

"The twins," we say in unison.

I hop off my perch and stretch to fetch my phone from the chair. Where is it? Four bird chirp rings later, and I finally find my phone between the cushion and the tangle of clothes that we clawed off each other last night like we used to when we were first dating.

"Mom, what's wrong? Are the girls okay?"

Henry sits up and puts his head against mine so he can hear the conversation.

"I'm not uptight, Mom," I retort. "Well, we were having a good time." I can hear the twins babbling in the background. "Yes, Mom. Thanks for checking in. Okay, see you tomorrow. Kiss my babies for me."

I collapse back onto the bed. Henry follows. We let out a relieved sigh. He turns on his side and props his head up into his hand.

"Do you want to go home?" he asks, smoothing my hair away from my face.

"No, I don't. It's just . . . It's overwhelming how much I love them. We've been gone for two days, but I feel like we are going to miss something important. A new coo or a wink or a silly, crooked smile."

Come on, Izabel. Henry's been so patient and helpful over the last few months.

My feeling of detachment toward the girls and hopelessness for the future since the accident was such a low point, and he didn't judge any of it. He just kept reminding me it's all part of the healing process.

And now we're on this amazing getaway that he planned so we could be alone and reconnect, and you want to up and leave? To add to all my bullshit self-pity, I can't stop thinking about the guilt that's eating away at me for leaving the babies for a sex weekend. They're only ten months old. We shouldn't be away from them this long, not yet. They're too young. Okay, stop it now—this maniacal behavior is not sexy at all.

"Jones, this getaway is for you to have whatever your beautiful heart desires, and if that means going home, then that is what we will do." He flashes me his signature Henry smile.

I turn to face him and rub my thumb across his bottom lip.

"No, we deserve this anniversary weekend after everything we've been through." I push at his chest gently until he's flat on his back again, his mischievous grin challenging my next move. I swing my leg around his body and hover over him. As I stare longingly into his green eyes, my mind begins to wander again, and I'm overcome with horrific memories of the past year that I've desperately tried to erase from my mind.

Before I can stop myself, I blurt out, "If you ever almost die on me again, I'll kill you myself. You hear me, Rudolph?"

He lets out a soft chuckle and pulls me in until my forehead rests on his.

"I'm not going anywhere, my love. You're stuck with me forever."

I inch my way down his body until our chests meet. Sometimes I just need to feel the cadence of his heartbeat for reassurance that he is still with me. I have no desire to live a life without him and the twins. My life only makes sense with them in it. I'm so tired. As safe as I feel tangled in Henry's embrace, my dreams should be euphoric, but they are all too often haunted by the nightmare that was that horrifying day.

□ □ □

"Hey, baby . . . can you answer my cell? I'm in the tub."
I sink down into the bubbles and rub my swollen belly.

"You're going to have the best daddy in the world," I say to my stomach. "And in a few weeks, you get to meet him and fall absolutely in love with him, just like I did. And if he gets his way, which I'm sure he will, there are going to be many of you little babies running around in the future."

I let out a contented sigh. *My life is right on track. I'm exactly where I am supposed to be.*

"What are you grinning about, beautiful?" Henry says while leaning against the doorframe of the bathroom.

I give him a big, toothy smile. "Wouldn't you like to know?" I tease. "Who called?"

His mouth forms a rigid line. "Bo."

I roll my eyes. Bo and I never severed ties like I thought we would. He fell into a bit of a downward spiral a couple of years ago. Part of me felt responsible, and so I kept going to his rescue. Henry never once questioned my intentions; he's always been supportive and eventually forgave Bo for what he did to me. He says everyone deserves a second chance. Henry convinced Bo that it would be beneficial to his therapy and recovery to volunteer at the shelter for battered women where his mother, Tippy, is a board member.

The Christmas holidays were especially hard on Bo. His younger sister, Becky, got married late December after a very quick engagement. Mind you, any engagement seems quick after what Bo's father, Jack Carmichael, put us through during our relationship. He made us change the wedding date three times. There was always a last-minute political event that was more important. We were engaged for three years before we got married. But Jack wanted this guy to be part of the family so badly. He's some hotshot political up-and-comer he wanted to dig his claws into, another minion. Bo took it really hard when his father pushed him aside for this new pet project. Henry and I were invited to the wedding by Tippy. It's up for debate whether it was for show or because she's genuinely thankful for the emotional support we still offer Bo. We declined the invite, of course. Adding insult to injury doesn't help anyone.

"What does he want now?" My third trimester hormones are apparent in the clipped tone of my query.

"The usual," Henry says. "He's drunk at a bar. I'm going to pick him up before he gets himself into trouble again."

I motion for him to sit at the edge of the tub and hold out my hand. He sits and envelops my hand in his and kisses my knuckles.

"You're so good. Have I told you lately what a lucky girl I am?" I swoon.

"Not nearly enough," he says, then leans down for a kiss.

I wrap my arms around his neck, almost pulling him in.

"Easy, tiger." Henry releases a hearty laugh.

"Babe, I can't help it. I read that during this stage of pregnancy, women get really horny, but this is crazy. I want you all the time. It's maddening."

He can't hide the amusement from his face. "Listen, I promise when I get home, you can take complete advantage of me," he says, kissing the tip of my nose.

"Are you mocking me, Mr. Rudolph?" I cast him a playful scowl.

"I wouldn't dare think of it, Dr. Jones. Plus, if the

only thing I have to complain about in my life is that my gorgeous wife wants sex all the time, I could die tomorrow a happy man."

"Okay, well, give me one more kiss before you go. I'll behave. Promise."

He blows me a kiss in consolation. "I'll be back in an hour, tops."

"I love you!" I yell out after him.

"Love you more. See you in an hour," he replies.

□ □ □

I wake with a start and bolt up to a sitting position. I am alone in bed. I panic.

"Henry! Henry!" I cry out.

He comes running into the bedroom. "Izabel, I'm here. I'm here." Henry sits on the bed and wraps me in his arms.

"Shhhh." He rocks me back and forth for comfort. "Come. I made breakfast. Let's eat, then we will head back home. You'll feel better then."

My breathing slows, but I clutch him tighter and kiss his bicep. I need to feel his flesh.

"I love you, Henry."

"I know," he says and kisses the top of my head. He stands and pulls me to my feet. "It's your favorite: egg whites and spinach," he singsongs.

"Ugh." I stick out my tongue. "Any bacon?"

"Hey, you were the one who said you have to lose five pounds and told me to ignore any insults directed at me to keep you on track. I'm just doing what I'm told."

He reciprocates by sticking his tongue out. Then he pulls me in and grabs my ass.

"I happen to love this ass and don't think you need to change a thing. But I will do whatever makes you happy."

"You know what would really make me happy right now? Getting a jump start on working off a few of those pesky pounds." I slide my right hand down the front of his low-hanging pajama pants and thank him with a generous squeeze and a few strokes.

He moans. "Yeah, fuck breakfast," he says and throws me on the bed.

□ □ □

We usually drive the scenic route back home whenever possible. There is so much history in the towns we pass through along the way, and at this time of year, the parks and civic centers are already decorated with the autumn holiday colors. Sometimes we'll stop in one of them to go to a farmers' market and grab some delicious pumpkin and apple pies.

The first time I took Henry to Milwaukee to visit Mom, we stopped in Wind Point to explore the lighthouse, and he immediately fell in love with the area. Once we got engaged, we started looking for a home here. Mom was of course beside herself, to say the least, when we told her how close we were going to move to her. Ultimately, we ended up buying our house with the in-law suite. I'd never seen her happier than when we showed Mom her new space. Henry and I agreed that keeping the condo in Chicago was a good idea because we both still worked in the city. We haven't spent much time there since the twins were born, but I think after this weekend, Henry will lobby to come more often. I reach across the middle console of the car and intertwine my fingers with his and give him a little squeeze. He turns to me and flashes me that smile. The smile that tells me everything is okay.

We continue down the colorful, tree-lined driveway towards the house. Sometimes I can't believe we own such a beautiful home on waterfront property. I feel bad that the family we bought it from went into foreclosure, but it was such a good deal that we couldn't pass it up. Henry made a huge donation to USA Cares, a charity for veterans, to help alleviate my guilt. The front of the house is newly decorated with a scarecrow and some cornucopias. Looks like Mom's been busy while we've been gone. This woman never stops. I hope I'll be half as good of a mother as she is.

Excitement builds as we reach the house. I look over at Henry, and he's grinning from ear to ear. I wiggle and clap my hands together.

"Happy to be home?" he asks, chuckling.

I can't even speak. I nod like a bobblehead.

"You're so amazing, Jones. Thank you for this weekend. We needed it. Now let's go kiss our babies."

"Yippie!" I squeal.

2

I run through the front door. Henry follows with our bags in hand. I hear the slap of their little hands across the hardwood floor as they round the corner. Hope finds us first. She is always first at everything. She needs to be held first and fed first. Hope is a little high strung. Henry jokes she is exactly like me, lovingly of course. She babbles as she makes a beeline for me at Mach speed in her half-crawl, half-downward dog position. She's so eager to walk. I won't be surprised if she is running marathons before her first birthday.

I scoop her into my arms and smother her little face with kisses. Then Faith peeks her head around the corner, moving at her usual leisurely pace. Of course I love my daughters equally, but there is something about Faith. Every time she flashes me her gummy little grin, my heart skips a beat. It must be because she is so much like Henry. They are one and the same. Those two are content sitting together for hours reading storybooks. She's always smiling, and she rarely cries. I often find them cuddled up, napping, their matching pouty lips parted just slightly while they breathe. I sit and watch them sometimes and reflect on how lucky I am to have them.

"Come on, baby," I encourage her.

Henry drops the bags and moves in closer, closing the distance. He squats down and claps his hands together. "Come to Daddy, Faith," he sings.

She lets out an excited screech, and the sound of her little hands slapping on the floor gets closer. Henry effortlessly lifts her with one hand and holds her like a football. That's her favorite position. She looks so minuscule in his arms. Being preemies, the twins are small to begin with, but because Faith came out second, she is a little smaller than Hope.

Mom makes her way down the hall, and to my surprise, Natalie is following her.

"Hey, Nat. I didn't think you could make it this weekend." When Henry and I planned our little getaway, I had asked Nat if she could help Mom with the twins. She really did want to help, but she had clients to entertain. When she said "clients," she put the word in air quotes, so who knows what she was really up to this weekend. I stopped asking questions a few air quotes ago.

"Are you kidding me? I can't go an entire weekend without seeing my goddaughters. I got here yesterday. We drank wine and gossiped all night. Isn't that right, Mumsie?"

Mom rolls her eyes.

"Did we have any cereal incidents this time, Nat?" I regard her questionably.

"You know, you let a baby eat cereal off the floor once, and you never live it down." She flips her arms above her head in defeat.

Henry takes Hope from my arms and smothers her

little angelic face with kisses too. She grabs hold of his hair and giggles with delight.

"I'll leave you ladies to chat." As he walks by, he kisses Mom's cheek and thanks her.

The three of us watch him admiringly as he walks into the next room. We all love him for different reasons and yet for the same reason.

"So how was your fuck-romp weekend?" Natalie blurts out.

My poor mom immediately covers her ears. She definitely does not need to hear this.

"Natalie!" I scoff in horror.

"What? We're all adults here. We all know that's what happened." She shrugs in her matter-of-fact way.

Mom shakes her head and rolls her eyes again. "I think I will go help Henry with the girls. You two can catch up all you want."

"Seriously, Nat, a filter and some discretion every now and then would be nice," I say, grinning.

"Look at you. You got banged so good this weekend, you can't even be mad at me." She leans forward and gestures a far-too-realistic hip thrust, making me blush.

"Admit it." She laughs.

"Okay. Fine. You got me. Yes, it was mind blowing." I reflect dreamingly on the last forty-eight hours. "But you're not getting any details. Sex with my gorgeous, animalistic, incredible lover of a husband is off limits to you. I know what goes into Nat's spank bank, and I prefer not to be in there." I give her a wicked grin.

"Don't forget I already know he's hung like a horse, and that, my friend, is indeed in my spank bank," she says, biting her knuckles.

I shake my head at her. I don't make a habit of discussing the size of my husband's penis, but one day when Natalie was visiting for the weekend, she happened to cross paths with him while he was getting out of the shower. It was priceless. Her jaw literally hit the floor, and she retreated to her bedroom in utter embarrassment. It was a while before she could look at him straight in the face without blushing. Now it's a running joke between the two of them. Every now and again, she will tease him to flash her a peek so she can assure herself that she still likes men. He doesn't, of course, but I know he's secretly flattered and proud of his manhood.

"OMG. Wait until you see the gifts I brought the girls. You are going to love it. Well, I love it, and that's all that matters." She two-steps up the stairs to the spare bedroom that she has claimed as her bedroom.

It's like having a third child when Nat comes to visit. A third child who drinks, smokes, and has a vulgar mouth. But I do love her just the same.

I take the opportunity alone to check out my ass in the hallway mirror. I twist my body and strain to see behind me. Damn you, five pounds.

"Aha, I caught you," Natalie accuses as she makes her way back down the stairs.

"Seriously, Jones, you're a fucking babe. You know how many women who haven't had kids who wish they had a rocking body like yours? Give yourself a break. Plus, you can't tell me that Henry doesn't love that Kardashian ass you've got going on."

I give her a shy shrug and pout.

"What's in the bag?" I pivot.

She pulls out two pink baby tutus and matching black leather jackets. I could easily say no way, no how, but the truth is the outfits are adorable. Everything Natalie does for my girls comes from the heart. They have such a special bond, given everything she's done for my family. Natalie was by my side and theirs when we really needed her. I can always find comfort in her words: *I may not be able to solve your problems, but I promise you you'll never have to face them alone.*

"Well?" she asks, swaying the clothes back and forth on the hangers.

I give her a kind, appreciative smile. "They're great, Nat. The girls will look so cute in them. Next time we visit the city, they will be wearing them."

"Hey, what's up?" Natalie's voice is full of concern. She hasn't lost her knack for reading my mind. She pulls me into a hug. "Listen. It's all good now."

I sigh. "I know."

The doorbell rings and we both jump. We look at each other and start laughing at our sappy interlude.

I open the door, and there is a delivery man standing there with a huge bouquet of flowers.

"Delivery for Izabel Jones."

I look quizzically at Natalie. She shrugs, indicating that she has nothing to do with it. She pushes by me and snatches the bouquet from the delivery man and flashes him her signature Natalie smile and a wink. "That's your tip," she teases. I offer my usual *sorry about her* apologetic smile and I shut the door.

"They're beautiful. I wonder who they're from." I unhook the envelope from the stem and pull out the card.

Happy fifth anniversary to a wonderful couple. To many more.

~Tippy xx

I look at Natalie and drop to my knees. She kneels next to me and grabs my hand. "I haven't heard from her since . . ."

Natalie squeezes my hand tight. "That night still haunts me, too, Jones."

3

My fingers are pruned. I guess it's time to get out of the tub. After I dry off, I slather my skin with cocoa butter cream. I read in some magazine that if you do this every day while you're pregnant, your skin will bounce back after the baby is born. When I finish, I look like I am wearing a cream jumpsuit. Hmmm . . . maybe a little overkill. I take my moisturizer out of the cabinet and apply a generous amount to my face and neck. Mom merits her flawless skin to always using a good moisturizer, morning and night.

I wasn't expecting to have alone time tonight. What should I do? Dealing with Bo always takes more than an hour. Maybe I'll watch one of the chick flicks that Henry always says he doesn't mind watching with me, even though I know he'd rather be watching sports. He's so good like that. We do everything together. I know some therapists think that in order to maintain a healthy relationship, one still needs to have individuality. Well, they clearly haven't met me and Henry because we dispel that theory completely. We keep each other in check; actually, he keeps me in check, balanced. If my ideas or anxieties start to get a little too atmospheric, he's my reality barometer.

I cozy up in the love seat and wrap myself with the throw blanket—our throw blanket. It's the same one we used the first night we spent together. Natalie had no objections with me taking it. Her comment was something about man jizz and sex smell. I ignored her, as usual.

The condo phone rings, interrupting my movie search.

I stretch across to the table and pick up the receiver. "Hello."

"Good evening, Dr. Jones. It's James from security. There is a Miss Spencer to see you. Should I let her up?"

I hear Natalie in the background shouting at him. He was bound to get the wrath of her at some point. "James, don't be a douche. I'm here all the time. You know who I am."

"Thank you, James. You can let her up."

Natalie often shows up unexpectedly, but this seems late for her. I wonder what's happened now. I unlock the door so she can let herself in and get back into my cozy position. Maybe I can convince her to watch the chick flick with me. What was it she said to me last time I asked her to watch one? "Jones, these lame-ass movies are a way for Hollywood to generate money from lonely women by perpetuating a fairy-tale life that doesn't exist." She's so cynical. Anyway, I'm living proof that a real-life fairy tale can exist.

"Hey, fatty—I mean, beautiful pregnant lady," Natalie chirps when she opens the door.

"Nice, Nat. What's up? Saturday night at eight, and you're not out at the latest and greatest.

What is the world coming to?" I tease.

"What? I can't just come by and hang with my best girl?" Her response is not convincing at all.

"Uh-uh, not buying it. Spill the beans," I probe.

"Where's Henry?" she asks, trying to avoid answering me.

"Okay, we'll play it your way first. But if you really need to know, he went to fetch Bo from a bar again."

She rolls her eyes with contempt. Natalie isn't as tolerant with Bo as Henry and I are. She doesn't understand why we continue to help him.

"Why do you even bother with that jerk-off?" she sneers.

"Natalie, be nice. He's had a rough time. Helping him is the right and the kind thing to do. Now stop diverting. What's up with you?"

She begins to tell me about a love/lust triangle that she's gotten herself into. I don't know how this girl ends up in these precarious situations. Somehow she is having an affair with a married couple, but neither the husband nor the wife knows they are both sleeping with her. Complicated . . . yes. Confusing . . . yes. Only Natalie . . . of course.

I am so caught up with Natalie's artful circumstance that I don't realize how much time has passed. I check the clock on the TV that has been looping movie trailers this entire time. It's ten thirty. Bo must be in rough shape, but it's unlike Henry not to call and check in.

"Nat. One sec. I am going to call Henry to make sure everything is under control with Bo."

"Sure. I need to get some more wine anyway. I'm starting to sober up from all your moral fortitude."

"You'll thank me one day for being your constant voice of reason," I say, laughing as I dial Henry's cell number.

Straight to voicemail. *That's odd.*

I hang up and dial Bo's number. His goes straight to voicemail too. I try both numbers a few more times.

"Jones, what's wrong?" Natalie asks. "You look green. Gonna hurl again?" She mocks and pretends to stick her finger down her throat. "You vomit like a frat boy on a Friday night."

"They're not answering."

I stare at my phone, willing Henry to call me back to say, "Sorry I missed your call, baby."

"I wouldn't worry about it, Jones. Bo's probably wallowing in his beer and talking Henry's ear off."

I don't answer her. I just look at the phone, psychically taunting it to ring. It rings. *It worked, thank god.*

"Henry!"

"Izabel," says a quiet but stern voice on the other end, "it's ... it's Damien."

Why is Tippy's assistant calling me?

"There has been an accident. You need to come to Holy Cross Hospital."

My heart sinks into my stomach. I understand all the words he said—*accident, hospital*—but nothing is making sense. There must be a mistake. Blood rushes to my head as bile rises to the back of my throat. I gag to keep it down.

After a long pause, I finally manage to reply, "Damien, what's happened and where's Henry? Where's Bo?"

Natalie is now standing next to me. She looks confused, which I am sure is mirroring my own expression.

"Izabel, I don't know anything further. I'm sure it's not that bad. Please, Tippy asked me to call you." His tone is not comforting. I drop the phone and run into the bedroom to grab my purse.

"Jones!" Natalie yells out. "What's going on?"

I run back out with my purse. "I've got to go to the hospital. There has been an accident."

"Accident—what kind of accident?" she asks, panicked.

"I . . . I don't . . . Damien said . . ."

"Jones, I'll drive. You don't even know what you are saying."

"No, I'll drive. You've been drinking," I scold.

"Dude, I had one drink, but do what you gotta do," she shouts back.

I honestly don't know who's better off driving at the moment. My mind is riddled with every worst-case scenario. Is Henry hurt? Is Bo hurt and Henry is helping him? I hope I don't vomit right now. After breaking every driving law, twenty minutes later, we pull up in front of the hospital. I slam on the brakes and stop the car in the middle of the roundabout. We run to the entrance, leaving both driver and passenger doors wide open. A security guard yells at us that we can't leave the car there.

"Tow it!" Natalie yells back at him.

As I run down the hall holding my belly, I'm halted dead in my tracks when I'm face-to-face with Tippy. I've never seen her look this bad. Her hair is a mess. Her face is gray, and her eyes are red and swollen.

I quickly realize this is far worse than my worst-case scenario.

"Where are they?" I cry. Tippy can't answer me. She shakes her head and points down the hallway. Natalie accosts a doctor walking by. She grabs the clipboard out of his hand. "Henry Rudolph. Where is he?"

His eyes widen. "Are you his wife?" he replies with urgency.

"I am," I whisper.

"Come with me, Mrs. Rudolph." I'm not about to correct him and go into technicalities of my last name. I'm married to Henry. Of course I'm Mrs. Rudolph.

The doctor ushers me into a room. There must be ten doctors and nurses surrounding the table. Their scrubs are saturated with blood. Chaos fills the room. The beeping and buzzing sounds of the machines they have Henry hooked up to are deafening. I freeze. I can't move any closer. This has to be some kind of mistake. This has to be the wrong room.

"Mrs. Rudolph, your husband's been shot," one of the nurses says.

I pull away when she places her hand on my arm. I hear one of the doctors yell. "We're losing him!"

I watch as they rub the paddles of the defibrillator together and put them to Henry's chest.

"Clear!" I hear someone shout, and I see his body convulse off the stretcher. It makes me jump, and tears start to pour from my eyes. I know what the sound of that flat tone means. Every particle that is my world is deteriorating right before my eyes. The floor has turned into quicksand, and it's sucking me in. My lungs are filling with sludge.

"Clear!" someone shouts again.

The nurse from before comes over to me. "Mrs. Rudolph, we're going to need you to wait outside. Let me take you out." Her instructions are clear, but I can't fathom the magnitude of what's happening. Back in the hallway, Natalie and I lock eyes. The look of horror in hers is my undoing.

"Henry!" I let out a blood-curdling scream. "Henry!" I shout again. The pain is unbearable. The knife-stabbing pains consume me. Suddenly, I grab my swollen belly and begin to collapse.

Without hesitation, the nurse leaps forward and grabs me under my arms before I hit the floor. "Get a gurney STAT," she bellows. "Get her to the OR and page the OB on call."

The ceiling tiles start to float by me. The sounds of the squeaky wheels and sneakers shifting underneath me are buzzing in my ears. The muted voices muffled above me, heavy pants of breath thrashing down on me. Then everything stops, and I am blinded by the bright light above.

□ □ □

I'm woken by the sweet baby's breath of open-mouth kisses. Henry has the girls hanging upside down, swinging like little cherub crib mobiles overtop of me. The twins are giggling and grabbing for my face.

"Where's Mommy? Get Mommy!" The girls giggle harder as he swings them like little pendulums. The happiness these tiny bodies are able to evoke is celestial. Every human at some point in their life should be privileged enough to experience this splendor.

"I wasn't going to wake you, but I thought you'd want to help bathe the girls with me." He smiles at me lovingly.

"Mmm. I'm glad you did." I take Faith from Henry's grip and unleash my own kisses all over her. We fly up the stairs like baby airplanes. I hand Faith back to her daddy and run the big tub.

"Isn't that too much water for them?" he inquires with concern.

"I'm getting in too." I grin.

"Then I'm getting in too," he says, smiling from ear to ear.

I strip down first, then sink into the tub. My post-natal breasts float on the surface of the water. I catch Henry sneaking an appreciative peek. He winks at me. It's a perfect temperature for the babies. Henry passes me one baby at a time. We sit, waiting for Daddy to join us. He tears off his clothes with excitement. I watch and admire his every move, the way his muscles ripple, the way his dark waves of hair cover his face when he bends down to remove his pants. When Henry gets in, the water rises slightly, making a bit of splash. The girls let loose a harmony of giggles and begin to hit the water like bongo drums. I pass Hope over to Henry, and the girls continue to splash and squeal with delight.

After all the baby bits are washed and dried and all twenty toes are kissed and tickled, we dress them in matching pj's. I always do that. It's too adorable not to. Tonight's pj's of choice are lime green one-sies with a white bunny pattern, but the best part is the cotton puff on the bum. Henry sits in the rocking chair and pops Faith on his lap, then I hand him Hope.

He cuddles them in close and opens a book in between them. The girls get into their usual position. Hope has one little hand on Henry's cheek and Faith has one of her little hands palm down, resting on his chest. He reads to them every night before bed; even on the nights when I want to, he shoos me away. He's a bit of a baby hog that way.

I stand in the doorway and listen. He's so animated when he reads, adding expression and emotion to every word. I love those little lines around his eyes when he smiles.

I retreat to our room and catch up on my own reading.

Half an hour later, Henry walks into the bedroom. I peer up over the rim of my glasses and fold my book into my lap. He leans against the wall with his hip cocked to one side. "Hey, sexy, you come here often?"

I throw my glasses and book to the floor. "Oh, yes. I come as often as I can." I flip the duvet to the side and pat the mattress with the palm of my hand. "Get your sexy ass to bed now," I order playfully.

He slithers over to the bed and crawls up between my legs until his lips meet mine.

"In your professional opinion, Doctor, do you consider it a character flaw that I have no self-control around you?" He blows kisses down my neck, fueling my carnal appetite.

"Mr. Rudolph, in my professional opinion, if you did exercise self-control around me, I think I would have to tie you up and have my way with you."

"Dr. Jones, one might consider that an immoral use of your bedside manner. I, however, do not see it that way.

I completely encourage your dereliction of duty when it comes to your bedside manner with me." He bites down on the skin just above my right breast, sending tingles through my nipples.

"Just shut up and kiss me already." I pull his lips to mine, our tongues deep in each other, our teeth clattering. He pulls my leg up at the knee and rubs his cock against my inner thigh. I groan loudly. *Will I ever get enough? I want to devour him.*

"Lie on your back," I whisper into his ear. He loves when I tease him. Henry props up on his elbows and watches me lick and bite my way down his taut stomach, fanning my hair down over his groin and back up between his legs. His response is pleasing, and I yearn to experience his pleasure. I wrap my warm lips around his arousal. Henry releases a gratifying moan. Stroke after stroke, I take him deeper and faster. His fingers twist through my hair as he watches me feast on him. Swirling my tongue up from base to tip, I shear my teeth gently around his head.

"Fuuuckkk." A whisper escapes his lips. "Come up and kiss me."

With one final pop, I trail my tongue up his body until I am back at his lips, invading his mouth. I reach down and push his cock into me. He throws his head back, and I hear the sound of pleasure as he inhales through his teeth. I slide down onto him until I feel the glorious burn deep inside me. His hands grip tight around my hip bones. With every gyration, I feel the heated pinch building deep under my belly button. We're nose to nose, lips on lips. Our legs tangled around each other, existing as one. Our pace slows.

We stare deep into each other's eyes, every kiss and every breath diaphanous.

"Do you have any idea how much I love you? You are my heart and my soul, my entire being. You are my forever." His words are a Shakespearean lament against my lips.

His declaration sets off my release. "Henry," I hum softly. The love I feel for him is so intense, tears flow down my face. He kisses the droplets off my cheeks and tightens his embrace. Our bodies are flush, and with one final, tender kiss, he finds his own quiet release.

4

Morning chaos—it's the perfect start to my day. The girls are in their high chairs, finger painting the pureed squash I made for them. I seldom leave the house without some sort of slop or dried cookie on my shoulder, usually a combination of both. Mom has made it a routine to come up to the house every morning for breakfast with the girls, whether I'm going to the office to see patients or working on files at home.

After I completed my PhD, Dr. Kennedy offered me a fellowship. When the year was up, I stayed and built my practice at his office. Until the twins are older, I only see patients three days a week, and although I have a hard time leaving them behind, the drive into Chicago alone is welcomed.

Henry opened his own firm once we got engaged. He is able to do most of his work remotely, so he doesn't have to take the long commute in very often either. It wasn't even a discussion about him moving to Chicago with me. He said I should stay close to my mom, and once we found our house, the deal was sealed. I always wanted the gathering house for my family. Big enough to host all of our friends and family, but still cozy.

Somehow, we all end up in the same room for hours. There is space for everyone to have their own seat, but we manage to sit on top of one another. Now that's love.

His parents visit as often as they can, even before the twins were born. When they are all together, they get very loud. Henry's mother, Virginia, or "the General," as her children have always called her, is usually the ringleader of game nights. She insists on bringing all the junk food and many, many bottles of wine.

She says, "In competition, the win is only worth it if you've had to overcome obstacles." Her tactic always works, however, because we drink too much and lose every game. The brothers usually accuse one another of cheating, and the wives just sit back and enjoy the entertainment. Henry's sister, Portia, is never around. She met an über wealthy start-up guy a couple of years ago, and they were married within six weeks. They eloped while jet-setting around the world. The family wasn't thrilled, but they weren't shocked by the news. She called Henry a few weeks ago to let him know they were living on some island in the Aegean Sea. Although Natalie and Portia hadn't been together for some time, she still took the marriage news hard. From what I hear, Portia still sneaks in a visit to her once or twice a year.

First, we kiss the babies, and then Henry and I head out the door at exactly 8:00 a.m. with matching coffee mugs in hand. Pathetic, I know, but the *Kama Sutra* pages we flip through and have mastered bridge the gross amount of cutesy. Henry goes in late on Mondays so we can drive in together. We get to catch up on adult discussions and minutia like the price of gas and interest rates. Topics I couldn't care less about, but it's a nice break from Miss Spider and Baby Einstein.

I always lean against the door and watch him while he drives. His profile is rugged and manly, but flawless. The faint beginnings of crow's-feet connect a thin line across his cheekbones. He has a strong-but-perfect aquiline nose, and his square, upturned chin has the sexiest little dimple in the middle that I cannot resist sinking my tongue into every day when I kiss him. He could be speaking Klingon for all I care as long as I get to stare at him.

It was an easy drive today, light traffic. We pull up in front of my office with time to spare before my first appointment. I give Henry my ceremonial kiss and dimple lick before I get out. He lowers the passenger-side window, and I lean in to finish our goodbye.

"I see my last patient at five o'clock today." I pout because I know we won't be home before the girls go down for the night.

His lips form a compassionate smile. "Okay, babe. I'll be back to pick you up at six o'clock. Have a good day."

"You too. Love you."

He leaves me with his irresistible wink as he drives off, the wink that makes me wet instantly every time. *Damn you!* He knows exactly what he's doing. I squeeze my legs together at the knees to divert my sensation. I take the stairs up to my office to burn off my sexual energy. Ten flights aren't so bad, even in three-inch heels.

When I walk through the fire exit door, I'm greeted by Dottie's smiling face and a "Good morning, love" in her magnetic Scottish accent. Dottie has been my assistant since I started my practice. She's great, very matronly in a fifties housewife kind of way. She is stuck in a bit of a time warp. Every time I see her, she is wearing a new polka dot tea dress and is adorned with blood red nails and pink lipstick. Dottie's not only an office assistant; she's my life assistant too. She has gone above and beyond any job description for me and my family over this past year.

"Good morning, Dottie. Did you have a nice weekend?" I chirp.

"Yes. Thank you, Dr. Jones, but we can claver later. Right now your Mr. Smith is early and waiting in your office for you."

Over the years, I've learned how to speak Dottie and understand her Scottish colloquialisms. *Claver* is the word she uses for "gossip." One day we were chatting, or clavering, between patients and she asked me why I go by Dr. Jones and not my married name. I answered, "Because I'm the one who received a doctorate degree, not my husband." That made her blush and laugh.

"Dottie, please call me Izabel," I plead. I feel awkward that she addresses me so formally because she's older than my mother. I guess it's a respect thing for me. I should be calling her Ms. Stevens.

"Oh, Dr. Jones, you know I can't do that," she tsks in her thick Scottish accent.

I smile with defeat. "Very well, Dottie."

She points towards the door of my office with the eraser end of her pencil. I look at my watch and sigh.

A two-hour session, and he's early.

"Hold my calls, please," I say and shut the door behind me.

At 6:10 p.m., I walk through the lobby's revolving doors. Henry is waiting outside, leaning against the car. He looks different than he did this morning. He's wearing a navy pinstripe suit and tie and a three-quarters-length camel cashmere dress coat. That's odd; he didn't mention he was going shopping today. I stop short to admire him. My man is absolutely gorgeous, and there's that look again that makes me weak in the knees. As I regain my clarity, I walk towards him, grinning.

"Well, well, Mr. Rudolph, to what do I owe this exceptional greeting?"

"Dr. Jones, you're crushing me." He grimaces. "How soon you forget. You use me for a sex-filled weekend, then toss me away."

I grab his face between my hands and suck on his pouty bottom lip. "Of course I haven't forgotten, but I thought we were just going home to celebrate our anniversary with the girls."

He slides his hands down to my behind. "Nope! You're all mine tonight. I spoke with your mother. She is going to sleep in the main house because I plan on getting you home well past curfew."

"Is this new outfit an anniversary gift to you?" I grab the knot of his tie and wiggle it.

"Yes, but that's not all." He reaches into the car through the window of the passenger side and pulls out a Nordstrom bag.

My eyes light up. "For me?" I squeak.

"Yes." He mimics my excitement by shaking the bag. "Why don't you run back in and change? Our reservations aren't until seven."

"Okay!" I squeal and skip back to the building.

"Do you need any help?" Henry shouts after me.

I look back at him and stick out my tongue. "No way. You stay right there. You're too distracting as it is."

I head back up to my office to use the private washroom. Dottie has left for the day, so I won't be delayed by chitchat. I tear into the tissue paper and touch the sapphire blue chiffon, admiring the most striking fit-and-flare dress, and of course a pair of nude Cuban-heel stripe stay-ups. Henry's favorite.

I look for the tag on the inside to see what size he bought, but it's been removed. That bugger. His theory is if it fits and you look good, why should the size matter? I scowl at his audacity, but more so at the fact that I know it will fit perfectly and look amazing. I slide the stocking up one leg at a time, then shimmy into the dress. The back is a low V-cut, luckily just above my bra strap. Although I don't think I would offend anyone if I went bareback. My new postnatal tits really are spectacular. Who knew I would like having big ones so much. However, tonight the girls are staying strapped in. I give my hair a quick finger tease and apply some fresh makeup, and I am ready to go.

I walk back outside twenty minutes later. I've left my coat open purposely so Henry can get a good glimpse at the dress before we get in the car.

He eyes me both lovingly and with pride in his purchase. I give him a quick peck on the lips "The tag, huh?"

He shrugs unapologetically. "Does it fit?"

I roll my eyes at him as I slide into the passenger seat.

"Let's go then, sexy." Henry winks and shuts the car door.

When we drive off, I ask where we're going.

"I thought we'd go to Gus's Place."

"Yummy. I can't remember the last time I had a good steak. Ooh, I love those baby pickles." I clap my hands with excitement.

Henry releases an amused laugh. "Baby, you make me laugh."

"What? Why are you laughing at me?"

"You show the same enthusiasm for baby pickles as you do for designer clothing. That is one of my favorite qualities about you. You're always happy." He reaches across and takes my hand into his and lifts it to his mouth, grazing his teeth against my knuckles.

"Well, I have three incredible reasons in my life to always be happy," I coo.

I feel his adoring smile on my hands.

"Oh, by the way, happy anniversary," I say as I lift my dress and expose my panty-free crotch. Henry fixes on my area and gasps. When he looks back up, he swerves to avoid the rumble strips on the shoulder of the road.

"Jesus, Jones, are you trying to get us killed?" He holds his hand to his heart, and I giggle.

When we arrive at the restaurant, we are cordially greeted by the maître d' at the front entrance of Gus's.

The maître d' nods. "Good evening, sir," and then he faces me, "madame. Do you have reservations with us this evening?"

"Yes. The name is Rudolph."

"Of course. Please follow me, sir. The rest of your party is here."

I look quizzically over at Henry. "Who else is here?"

"You'll see," he teases.

We follow the maître d' through the maze of tables to the back of the room. I don't see anyone I recognize, and we've covered the entire restaurant. *Where are we going?* I wonder.

We follow him down a staircase and then a narrow hallway. He opens a door at the end of the hallway and ushers us in with a bow. Henry slips him a tip inconspicuously with a handshake. I peek in and Natalie is sitting at the table with a man I've never seen before. She jumps out of her seat and picks me up into a Natalie hug and spins me. I hope I'm not flashing my under-the-dress nakedness to this stranger.

"Do you know how hard it was for me not to say 'See you tomorrow' when I left the house yesterday?"

"Um, Nat, who's the guy?" I whisper in her ear.

She fakes a laugh, pretending I just said something really funny. "That's Benjamin, but I'll tell you more later."

I look over, and Henry and mystery guy are shaking hands and making introductions.

The four of us sit at the table set up for us in the middle of the wine cellar. The room is rustic and has a faint musty smell that's barely obscene because the combination of pizza and garlic aromas is mouth-watering. It looks like what I imagine a century-old farmhouse lulled by rolling hills in Siena would look like. I pull Henry close and bestow a thankful smooch on his face for organizing this wonderful dinner.

It's a celebration we all hold right to. I even love that Benjamin is here. If he's passed Nat's test, that's all I need to know about him.

After a few niceties and small talk around the table, Henry and I start our speed-dating questions. We don't usually get this opportunity. With the exception of Portia, Natalie has never introduced a love interest to us before. We've come face-to-face with the occasional hello as we crossed paths with a stranger being ushered out midmorning, followed by Nat's final parting words: "It's been fun. I'll call you, babe."

Henry begins, "So, Ben, it's incumbent on Izabel and me to interrogate you, but I suspect you expected this would happen?"

Ben chuckles. "Of course. Please ask away."

"Okay, let's start with an easy one. What's your last name?"

"Hardy," Ben answers with excitement, anticipating the next question.

"What do you do, Benjamin Hardy?" I chime in.

"I teach art history here in Chicago at McMalvern High School."

"Are you from Chicago, Ben?" Natalie jumps in.

We laugh at her. "What? I was feeling left out." She pouts.

"My family is from Detroit originally, but we moved to Chicago after my grandmother died."

"I'm so sorry to hear that." I offer a sympathetic smile.

"Aw, thanks, Izabel, but it was many years ago now."

"So how did you and our girl over here meet?" Henry pinches Natalie's cheek and teases her.

She gives him an "I'm warning you" look.

"We were attending the same art auction," Ben continues. "I heard her before I saw her, and I knew at that moment I had to meet the face behind that roar of laughter." Ben smiles as if the fondest memory has occupied his mind.

"I have to be honest. It was a terrible first impression, she was brutal—rude and crass. At one point I thought she was going to punch me, but I persisted. There was something about her; she was irking me, and I needed to know more about this woman." Ben takes Natalie's hand into his and gives her knuckles a quick kiss.

Our attention is all his. Henry and I are gripped by his devoted recount of Natalie.

"'Persisted' is a word you could use, I guess," Natalie interrupts. "He followed me around the entire night like a lost puppy dog. He injected himself into every conversation I was having."

"Ah, yes, but my tactic worked because when I finally got the courage to ask you out, you said yes—actually you said, 'Fine, but only if you'll stop following me around.' And I think you called me a weirdo."

Henry and I applaud Ben for the accurate characterization of Natalie. I run the risk of sounding like her, but he must have a gigantic set of balls on him to have challenged her like that. I love him already.

As the night goes on, we enjoy learning more about Benjamin and his family and about his travels around the world, studying art. He's not condescending in the least, and he treats Natalie with the utmost respect and is so chivalrous. Natalie's usual response to a guy trying to push her chair in for her would go something like: "Dude, I have hands. Now back the fuck off." Not with Benjamin, though.

My cheeks hurt for her from all her smiling. We've finished our pre-drinks, appetizers, and a bottle of wine. I'm feeling a little tipsy already. Henry switches to sparkling water when he sees me pour my second glass of wine. He leans over and whispers in my ear, "This is your night to enjoy, my love."

He will always enjoy an after-dinner whiskey, though, a luxury he learned from his grandfather, Charlie. We're having a grand time, laughing and exchanging anecdotes. The atmosphere in the room is easy. The lights are dim and candles flicker on shelves around us. The conversation breaks into gender pairs. While the boys are talking hockey, I scoot closer to Natalie to get the new-man scoop.

"He's so cute, Nat. I love him already. What's the deal with you two?"

"Yeah, he's all right." Natalie's noncommittal response makes me laugh louder than I expect. Luckily, the men don't seem to notice.

"How many times have you guys gone out? And why didn't you say anything yesterday when you were at the house?"

"I was going to tell you, then the flowers showed up, and, well . . ." We look at each other and frown, and we know to quickly move on from the subject.

"I think he's lovely, and he seems really into you. You should bring him to our place for Thanksgiving dinner. He can hang out with the Rudolph men and watch football all day."

My eagerness to assimilate him into our gang is palpable. I have an instant connection with him. She acts like she doesn't care, but I know she would like to be in a committed relationship at this point in her life, with a man or a woman. Benjamin just happens to be the first person I've ever seen Natalie this happy with in a very long time. One hour, a fantastic steak dinner, and another bottle of wine later, and we're all delectably full. While there is chatter amongst the table about dessert and aperitifs, I excuse myself to go to the washroom. I am relieved to find a bathroom in the hallway, instead of having to take the maze back up the stairs to the main restaurant. I'm not convinced I would have found my way.

A few seconds later, there's a knock on the door. *It must be Natalie wanting to talk*, I assume. It's not like I mind her being in here when I go. She has seen me pee probably too many times unnecessarily in the last twenty years. I open the door to let her in. Henry grabs me and pushes his body against mine until he has me pinned to the wall. He sticks his leg out to shut the door behind him. I look at him with animated elation.

"When I picked out this dress for you today, I knew I wanted to fuck you in it." He follows with kisses that are passionate and desirous. I throw my arms around him and grab his behind. His full body weight is against me, so I can feel his hard cock against my belly. "Then when you showed me your naked pussy in the car, that's all I could think about all night."

Henry pulls at my hair and licks down the side of my neck. "Do you want me to fuck you, right here?"

The rumble of his moan on the tender skin behind my ear injects pleasure directly between my legs.

"Yes." My answer is urgent and wanting. I unbuckle his belt and then his button. I free his cock from his boxers and give it a generous squeeze and a few strokes. He turns me around so I'm facing the mirror. My hands are supported by the edge of the sink, and I spread my legs. He flips up the back of my dress and luxuriously slides two fingers into my readiness. I arch my back and push back onto his hand. His fingers slide out, then back in so slowly.

"Henry, I need you inside of me." I buck back onto his fingers and release a slow whine.

I reach behind me and take him in my hand and guide his cock between my legs. I rub my throbbing clit with his tip before I push myself onto him. He feels even bigger this way. I use the sink as leverage to keep the steady pace of backward thrusts. He reaches around between my legs and methodically fondles my wet, swollen spread. Our pace quickens, knowing our end is close. I let out a loud moan.

Henry leans closer to my ear. "Shush," he orders.

Our eyes meet in the mirror. He brings his fingers up to my mouth and slides them between my lips, urging me to taste my arousal. I fellate his fingers, and then bite down on them. The sound of his intense groans sets me off into an orgasmic spiral.

"I'm coming, Henry!" I cry.

He grabs my hips and drives into me one—two—three more times, then grinds his orgasm into me. He collapses onto my back and hugs me close.

"Mmm. I've been waiting to do that to you all day," he says, kissing the exposed skin on my back above the V-cut of my dress.

"Well, I'm glad I could oblige my sex god of a husband." I giggle.

He pulls out, making me wince. I hand him some paper towel to dab dry before he does up. "I'll always choose you over dessert. Now let's go enjoy a stiff Macallan before we head home." He kisses the tip of my nose.

"You go first. I need to take care of this mess first."

He mocks me with a shocked look of surprise and points to himself.

"Okay, baby. I'll see you back out there." He opens the door and peeks out like a guilty teenager before he leaves.

A few minutes later, I am back in the cellar. I avoid eye contact with Nat so she doesn't out us for our bathroom romp. Surprisingly, she doesn't even notice that I've returned; she's too interested in her conversation with Benjamin.

After a round of after-dinner drinks, we say our goodbyes out front of Gus's. Handshakes and hugs all around.

"I'll call you tomorrow," I say as I hug Nat.

"Yes. Lots more to talk about," she responds warmly.

The valet brings our car around. Natalie and Benjamin say a final goodbye and walk hand in hand down the street.

I nestle into my seat and kick off my shoes. We have a long drive home. Maybe I should've had an espresso so I can stay awake on the way. Henry doesn't mind the solo drive. He'll crack open a Red Bull, his one vice. He usually has one stashed in the middle console.

I'll listen to a podcast and sleep. *Dateline* is a go-to of mine. There's something soothing about the voices of the hosts, even though they're talking about missing persons and unsolved mysteries. Staying at the condo is not an option tonight. I want to be home for when the girls wake up in the morning. When Henry gets in the car, I turn to face him, and I hand him a box.

"What's this?" He looks puzzled.

"It's your anniversary gift."

"I think you've given me plenty of gifts in the last few days," he says, followed by a wicked grin and a wink.

"Just open it." The anticipation is killing me.

He tears away the wrapping and flips the lid of the box. He stares at it, then he registers what it is. "It's Charlie's watch. Where . . . ? How . . . ?" His confusion makes me laugh.

"Just put it on. Let's see how it fits."

"Izabel. This is . . . you are . . . you're amazing." He paused and looked at me, still a little stunned. "How did you do this?" When he smiles, I see that his eyes are twinkling with threatening tears.

"It took me a while, but Natalie helped. She knows some guy that knows a guy who owns an underground pawn shop, and there were whispers on the street that a vintage, inscribed Rolex with a gold face was hot and available. She made the introduction and . . ."

"Jones, did you meet this guy alone?" Henry inquires with worry.

"No. Are you kidding me? Natalie almost didn't let me go at all. She said that I'm a pushover and would be taken advantage of."

Henry gives me a smile that indicates he agrees with Natalie's declaration.

I roll my eyes at him. "Anyway, I explained to him what happened, minus a few tragic details, but she wasn't wrong because once I told the guy the watch originally belonged to the great American artist Charles Rudolph, his price went up. I had every intention of buying it back at any price, but Super Natalie got between us, and they exchanged some colorful words and bartered on some other deals. Before I knew it, she handed me the watch and said, 'Let's get out of here before he changes his mind.'"

"It's always an adventure with her," he says, admiring it on his wrist, and then he frowns. "This must have been so difficult for you, but we're not going to open the door on the past and what happened that night, right now. Only happy thoughts for our anniversary."

"I know how much it means to you, and you mean even more to me, so it only made sense to get it back."

"This is so incredible. Thank you so much, my love."

He bestows the most tender kiss on my lips. It makes my heart skip a few beats.

I stare deep into his eyes. "No, Henry, thank you. For everything."

Henry kisses me on the nose. "Enjoy your nap, sleepy head. We'll be home in no time."

5

"Izabel, honey, you have to listen to me, okay?"

I see the nurse from before standing over me. Her hair is pulled back in a messy ponytail hanging off to one side of her head. She's wearing light blue scrubs. I focus on the dancing cat pattern on her top.

"I have to do a quick ultrasound so we can see how your baby is doing." She pulls my T-shirt up and drapes a sheet over me.

"Please take care of my baby. Where is Henry? I need to see Henry." I try to get off the table, but a very tall male nurse with a scruffy reddish beard holds me down, sympathetically but with force.

"Izabel, you need to lie still so I can take care of your baby." The female nurse's voice is stern but soothing. I hear the squirt of the gel and then the cold blob hits my stomach. The nurse rolls the wand around my belly, up and over and then back down to the top of my pubic area.

"Izabel, the babies are in distress, and we need to do an emergency delivery." She looks over at the other nurse with concern. "Page the OB again. These babies have to come out now."

"What do you mean *babies*? I don't understand. I need Henry. Please . . ." I cry. "Somebody go . . . go get him for me." The male nurse puts an oxygen mask around my nose, and I feel the pinch of a needle go into my arm.

A dark-haired lady walks in. She's wearing a white lab coat over pink scrubs that look vibrant against her dark skin. A warm, prickly feeling starts running through my veins. I hear a muffled conversation somewhere in the room.

"Izabel Jones . . . Thirty-two-year-old female, twenty-nine weeks pregnant . . . twins . . . in preterm labor caused by traumatic stress."

The sounds are muted now, and everything around the room starts to move in slow motion. I fight to keep my eyes open and try to make sense of what everyone is saying.

"Husband was admitted with multiple gunshot wounds." The doctor looks up from my file with wide eyes, and the nurse responds with a slow blink and a shake of her head.

I want to scream out, but my vocal cords are failing me.

"Izabel, I'm Dr. Campbell," I hear a kind but stern voice come from the beautiful Black doctor hovering over me. Even through all the chaos, I take notice of how smooth her skin is and her lashes look like two butterflies on her eyes. "We're going to take care of you and your babies now." The two nurses roll me onto my side. "I need you to stay very still, honey. You're going to feel a bit of pinch."

The cold liquid is filling my body and tears roll down my face. *My Henry is gone.* In a blur, a white sheet gets yanked up negligently around my waist. There is nowhere to look now but up. I'm forced to stare up at the ceiling, and for a brief blip, I'm mesmerized by the cadence of the fluorescent bulbs that appear flickering at the speed in which the gurney is hurling down the narrowing hallway.

I turn and face the nurse and grab her hand. "Please. I can't do this alone. I need to see Henry." I babble through the oxygen mask.

"You won't be alone. I'll be with you the whole time." She wipes the tears and hair away from my face.

A drowned-out briefing comes from the other side of the sheet that I can't quite make out, but then I feel a pull in the pit of my abdomen and let out a deep drawl of a moan. Suddenly, the room is filled with commotion; people ascend in masks, moving from one side of the room to the other. There is a deafening beeping sound.

"Baby number one is out!" I hear someone shout. "One more tug. Okay, Izabel? You're doing such a great job."

Why don't I hear crying? I'm dizzy.

"Baby number two . . . let's go!"

The room goes black. No sounds. No lights.

No Henry.

□ □ □

"Hey, sleepyhead, we're home," he says, kissing my eyelids. I open my eyes wide and stare up at him.

I'm overcome with fear and shock once again. Henry knows not to ask. Reliving that day is hard for both of us.

He leans his forehead on mine and inhales deeply. "Come on. Let's get to bed."

When we're inside, I tiptoe into the twins' room and watch them sleep for a few minutes, their little chests moving softly up and down. I lean into their crib and give first Hope then Faith a gentle little kiss. Faith doesn't flinch, but Hope throws her tiny arms above her head and gives me a sleepy, half-cocked smile. This little one innately knows how to cheer me up, just like her daddy.

Back in our room, I kick off my shoes, slip off my stockings, and let my dress fall to the floor. I climb into bed and curl up into a ball in my usual spot next to Henry's side. Today was a rollercoaster of emotions, and I fall asleep before my head hits Henry's chest.

□ □ □

I look up from the twins resting in their stroller to see the sun is shining. Faith's giggle sounds almost like the cheery bird chirping in the distance as we crunch over the multicolored leaves. But the impending winds are blowing off the water, and I turn the double stroller towards me so the girls are sheltered from the wind.

It's been a week since Henry surprised me with our anniversary dinner. My mind is preoccupied with visions of our little romp in the bathroom as I sit on my bench on the pier, enjoying a coffee. I still need to catch up with Nat and get more out of her about her new man.

Oh, and when I say my bench, I mean it's literally *my* bench. When we moved to Wind Point, Henry's firm did some pro-bono work towards the revitalization of the waterfront. It was always beautiful, but the funds allowed for some really amazing upgrades. There are planter boulevards and interlocked pathways and a series of custom cedar-and-metal benches that face out towards the water along those pathways. My bench has a plaque on it with an inscription that reads: remember to smile. This is something Henry has always said to me over the years, through our good times and our bad. I try to take the girls on this walk daily if I can. When they nap, I sit and reflect on my life.

I by no means have a hard life and am extremely grateful for all my fortunes, but hardship is subjective, and I would not wish the shit that I've lived through this last year on anyone. It has taken a great deal of time for me to get back to this place in my head, but sitting here gives me clarity. The way the sunbeams dance off the water like miniature nymphs makes life seem so uncomplicated. Watching my babies sleep makes life seem uncomplicated, although there was a time not so long ago when these precious little gifts were the devastation of my mortal essence.

As I walk back up to the house, I see Mom standing at the top of the driveway. The look on her face is ominous, but I don't think much of it.

"Hey, Mom."

"Hi, darling."

"Do you want to come over to the swings with us? I want the girls to enjoy some more sunshine before it gets too cold out." I unbuckle Faith first and hand her to Mom.

"Darling, something came for you while you were out."

I play goo-goo ga-ga with Hope before I unbuckle her side of the stroller.

"What is it?" I ask without looking up. I'm too busy nuzzling my nose into Hope's belly. She's laughing and tugging at my braids. Mom doesn't answer. When I look up, I see the look of apprehension on her face.

"Mom—what is it?"

She hands me an envelope that I hadn't noticed she had been holding behind her back. "I wasn't sure if I should give this to you. I know you've been struggling a little this week."

I give her a look of confusion.

"A man driving a black Escalade delivered it."

I freeze. "Damien."

Mom's not wrong. I've had a hard enough time this week as it is, reliving horrors and trying to suppress emotions. Sometimes it pops up again, even after all this time.

What the hell does he want? First Tippy sends flowers. Now this? The last time I heard from Damien was the worst day of my life.

"I don't know if I can open this, Mom. It's too painful." I rub my forehead and pinch my temples.

"Oh, sweet girl, I wish I could take your pain away from you. Why don't I take the girls back up to the house, and you can have some time to yourself?" She puts Faith back in her seat and grabs the handles. I am despondent. I can't answer her. She starts to stroll the girls away and looks back at me.

"Darling, maybe the best way to forget something is to remember."

Her profound words make me frown.

All I do is remember. I watch them walk away. I'm still frozen. Is Mom right? Should I open Pandora's box? I can't go back to the purgatory that was my life. Every morning I wake up, I recall that day like an even more fucked-up version of *Groundhog Day*. Some days are better than others, and I force it down to the deepest part of my soul and don a fake smile. I wish I were stronger, like Henry. He sees life so clearly, as should I because we're so blessed. He makes his *live for today* theory seem so easy, but if he only knew how agonizing that day was for me maybe . . . No, I would never want him to feel the way I did the day my world fell apart. My hands shake as I tear open the envelope. I pause and close my eyes tightly. I'm not sure I want to read this. Inside is a handwritten note in Tippy's perfect cursive.

Izabel,

I hope this note finds you and your family well. I will keep this short. I want to inform you of the upcoming trial. Proceedings will begin December 16. I understand you and Henry have your own reasons for not pursuing legal action and have chosen not to press charges against the perpetrators, but it would be judicially beneficial if you would reconsider and attend. Jack and I believe if the jury is aware there is another victim present, that will work in our favor. Damien can send you further details if need be.

Best,

Tippy

Henry made the decision that it was best for our family that he didn't press charges because he didn't want that night to define our life. He said they will be prosecuted accordingly for what they did to Bo. The nightmares that haunt me in the daylight are difficult enough to contain, and Tippy's reminder puts me over the edge. I drop the letter to the ground and fall into a downward spiral of vehement fury as all my worst memories come flooding back.

6

"Where are my babies? Why can't I see them?"

My mind is groggy; my mouth is dry and pasty. I'm so cold, and my body is shivering. I try to lift my hand to remove the oxygen mask, but my body is completely numb. There is a faint nagging pain in my stomach. I blink a few times as I focus in on the nurse looking down on me.

"Izabel, honey, you gave birth to two girls. We had to take them up to the neonatal unit. They will take good care of them up there. They are having a little trouble breathing on their own, and their blood pressure isn't as good as we want it to be."

"Wait, what? Are they going to be okay?"

"Yes. This is common practice with premature deliveries. We will get you up there soon." The nurse turns to walk away. I find the strength to lift my arm and grab her hand.

"Please take me to see my husband," I beg.

She stops and looks down at me with grace and squeezes my hand. "I'll see what I can do, love." Then she walks out of the room.

What seems like hours later, I'm wheeled into what I can only assume is a recovery room.

I am alone. I don't know anything. I have no awareness, physically or mentally. And there is a knock on
the door. Natalie peeks her head in cautiously.

"Hi. Can I come in?" she asks softly.

I nod, but seeing her triggers my mental state, and I
shatter. She rushes to my side.

"Tell me what to do."

"Henry," I manage to say through my sobs. And
with that, Natalie is out the door.

I hear commotion in the hallway and then hear Natalie yell, "Take her to see her goddamn husband now,
or I'm going to start unplugging important shit."

She comes back a few minutes later with my nurse.
The nurse checks the bag that hangs above me on the
metal rod, unhooks something, then places the bag
beside me on the bed. Then she starts to roll my bed
across the room and doesn't once let up on the disapproving look she's giving Nat.

Normally I would be mortified by Nat's behavior,
but right now, if I could, I would jump on her and hug
her.

"You stay here," the nurse scolds as she looks over
at Natalie, who is leaning against the wall, presumably
proud of herself for getting her way.

"Uh-uh, Nurse Ratched, I'm not leaving her side,"
she counters.

The nurse rolls her eyes in defeat, and we all start to
move. The fluorescent lights race overhead as we speed
down the hallway. Doctors and nurses barking orders,
patients moaning and crying, the sounds carve at my
ears like a sharp knife. Then we stop. I hear the chime of
the elevator. She wheels the bed in straight to the back.

After another elevator chime, we are back on the move. Wherever we are, it's much quieter now. The voices are soothing and soft. The lights are dim.

We come to a full stop, and I hear the nurse say, "Okay, missy, this is as far as you go. You can see her again when she's back in her own room."

Without protest, Natalie leans down and kisses the top of my head. I see her give the nurse the "I'm watching you" finger gesture. The nurse moves to the foot of my bed and opens a door. She pulls me into a room. It's quiet, too, but the weak sounds of the machines and beeps are deafening. The nurse positions my bed parallel to the wall and opens the curtains. Then I see him.

"Henry." I gasp and immediately try to get up. The nurse holds me down.

"Izabel, you have to stay in your bed, or we'll have to go."

I nod in defeat and exhaustion. She helps me turn to my side so I can face him.

"Is he . . . will he?"

I can barely get the words out of my mouth. Seeing him lying there still is too surreal. This shouldn't have happened. This is Bo's fault. The slow burn of rage is annihilating my core. I hate that I'm angry. Pain and sorrow are the only emotions that should control me right now. Hatred won't help Henry. If he were awake, he would only find kind words for Bo. I have to do the same, or we'll never get through this.

"He's in an induced coma. The doctors were concerned with a trace amount of swelling in his brain. We'll learn more about his injuries once the sedation is turned off."

"When will that be?" I can't hide the desperation in my voice.

"We'll know more tomorrow. The attending doctor will come and speak with you then. I'll give you a few minutes alone." She regards me sympathetically. Then she leaves the room.

I reach for his hand, but I am still too far to touch him. I shimmy closer to the edge of my bed and strain as I stretch toward him. The shooting pain in my abdomen is nothing compared to the pain in my heart. With his hand finally in mine, I begin to cry. His usual olive complexion is now gray. His lips, his beautiful lips, are dry and cracked. There's a tube sticking out of his mouth and taped to his chest; it's attached to a horrific-sounding machine that makes his chest puff up, then collapse again. There are gauze patches on his left shoulder and his stomach. Both with a faint blood stain at the surface.

"Oh, Henry, you can't leave me. You have baby girls who need you. *I* need you."

My convulsive sobs surface from the deepest part of my belly. "I can't do this alone. Please come back to me."

A few minutes later, my nurse comes back in with another nurse.

When she gets to my side, she strokes my arm. "It's time to go, Izabel."

"No, please, he needs me here. You don't understand. He knows I'm here."

She looks over at the nurse who is checking Henry's connections and wounds. She nods and smiles.

"Okay, Izabel, the medicine should wear off, and

you should be able to stand on your own in about an hour. Then I will take you to see your girls. You can stay here until then."

"Thank you. Thank you. You're such a good person, and when Henry wakes up, he's going to tell you about karma and cosmic principle and all the stuff I usually roll my eyes at him about when he . . ." I babble inarticulately.

The nurse squeezes my hand and smiles.

"I'll be back in an hour. Stay in your bed," she orders kindly.

I am able to wiggle my toes again. That means my time is almost up. This is turning into a bittersweet moment. It's not right that I have to make this decision. I have to leave my comatose husband to go see my babies in synthetic wombs because my body decided not to care for them any longer. No sooner have I finished my thought than my bearer of bad news returns. Maybe if I squeeze his hand tighter, she won't take me away from him.

"It's time to go. Your babies need you too." She walks over to my bed and unlocks the wheels.

"Can I come back later? I'll need to be here when he wakes up in the morning."

The nurse cocks her head to the side. Her expression is pacifying.

"Let's see how you do after you see your girls."

She wheels me back towards the door. My heart is beating double-time from anxiety . . . depression . . . sorrow. As we travel down the hallway again towards the elevator, I am struck with the realization that I have yet to ask about Bo. Is he okay? Was he hurt?

Was he the one who brought Henry in? I swallow down the big lump that's obstructing my windpipe and take a deep breath.

"Do you know what happened to the other man who came in with my husband? Bo Carmichael?" She doesn't answer right away. "He's my ex-husband. They were together tonight."

"I don't know, dear. Let's get you settled with your babies first, and then I'll find out for you."

I reach for her hand that's resting on the safety rail of the bed. "Thank you," I whisper.

We finally arrive at the hospital's neonatal wing. The hall appears endless. Just as it would seem we reached the end, it would stretch even farther, making the transfer here excruciatingly long. Eventually, the nurse parks the bed against the wall and lowers the rails. With her assistance, I sit up. I wince at the incision's pain now that the medicine has worn off. I flip my legs off the bed and lower myself to the ground. I feel shaky and weak, a combination from both my pain and sorrow and everything else I've had to experience tonight. She takes my arm in hers for support and ushers me into the room.

All of the other nurses in the room are dressed in pastel-colored scrubs. Some with a kitten pattern, others with a diaper-pin pattern. The ambient lighting is a dull pink that transitions from light to dark down the walls. As I look around the room, I see the row of glowing blue baby pods lined up against the walls. We walk slowly over to one of the incubators. I haven't allowed myself to be happy about the arrival of these unexpected precious gifts that Henry and I created.

It's as if I'm looking down onto a figment of a snow globe, watching these two tiny, little bodies lying next to each other, swaddled in yellow blankets and matching little hats. I gasp when I see the tubes taped around their tiny mouths and noses. The nurse places her hands gently on my shoulders.

"You can touch them."

"I don't want to hurt them." I frown.

"You won't." The nurse gently laughs. "They need to feel your touch. Just put your arms through the holes here." She points to the holes at the side of the incubator. I carefully insert my hands into the inverted gloves attached to the pod. Hesitantly, I reach for their twiglike legs. I cautiously rub my thumbs up the instep of their itty-bitty pink feet. The feeling I had the first time Henry touched my arm years ago in the coffee shop comes rushing back like a lightning bolt. How are these two little bodies able to induce such a divine strength? Instantly I fall completely and madly in love with them, and I know I will spend the rest of my life protecting my precious little gifts. I am overcome with happiness. Tears of joy spill down my face. My spirit and will have been resurrected.

"Congratulations on your baby girls," the nurse offers. "What are their names?"

I swing my head to look at her. "I don't know. We hadn't decided on one. Now there are two. I'll name them when Henry wakes up," I say optimistically. The nurse lowers her eyes and walks away, leaving me alone with the girls and a slight feeling of unease. I will not be discouraged; from this point forward, I will only believe in the positive. I have to—for the girls, for me, for Henry.

7

As I sit on a chair in front of the glowing blue pod caressing the girls, I can't help but worry about the other babies that are in the NICU. Even in the midst of my own horrific anguish, the thought of the devastation the other mothers must feel leaves a heavy blight on my heart. It's not fair. These poor innocent beings have no control over how they were brought into this world, and already they have to endure what most adults would not be able to handle. I immediately feel a connection with all of them and hope that I can offer even a minuscule amount of support in their time of frailty. I've been told that my girls are stabilizing better than expected and that they'll be able to move into my room with me in the next hour.

I almost have my nurse convinced to move us all into Henry's room. I may have told a little fib that I've done extensive research on how some comatose patients respond to external sounds and conversations. That it would be extremely beneficial for Henry to have me and the girls there to speed up his recovery. I did read that in an article in the *Psychiatric Times*. But I would tell her a unicorn flew down from the sky and sprinkled the message at my feet if I thought it would help.

I'm so exhausted, but running on adrenaline and hope. I glance at the clock. It's 4:30 a.m., and I fight to keep my eyes open, refusing to succumb to the darkness. Getting into Henry's room is my goal before I even consider laying my head down, even if it takes another twenty-four hours. I'm getting used to touching the babies through the gloves and having fun with them now. I've given them little nicknames. Baby number one has a light pink hue to her skin, so I call her Babe, like the baby pig from the movie, and baby number two has the tiniest little dimple on her chin just like her daddy, so I've named her Little Rudi. When Henry took me to meet his parents for the first time, his mother told the obligatory stories, as mothers do, to embarrass their child in front of a love interest. She pulled out the photo albums and boasted lovingly at his baby photos. She said they called him Little Rudi until he was about nine years old because he was so much smaller than the other two Rudolph brothers.

It will be such a special moment when Henry meets his daughters. He, too, will fall madly in love with them. The nurses told me it's okay to move them around now. They said it's best to touch them as much as possible, especially because they should be living inside of me for another eight weeks at least. I turn Babe on her side, then Little Rudi, so they are facing each other, and right before my eyes, I witness the most magnificent sight. They stretch out their little arms and hold on to each other's hands. This is exactly the sign I needed to reinstate my faith. Even with everything that's happened today, I can't help but be filled with joy. A smile creeps in, covering my face from ear to ear.

I peek over with tear-glistened eyes to my nurse, who has just come back into the room, and right behind her is Natalie so close on her heels they might as well be wearing the same pair of shoes. I can tell by the look on the nurse's face that Natalie has become her biggest pain in the ass of all time. For the first time since I landed on the doorstep of this dreaded building, I smile when I see Natalie. I'm excited for her to meet the babies.

I'm just about to share my revelation with them when I see a tall, older, gray-haired man wearing a white lab coat saunter in behind, as if on a well-trodden path. His white skin is sullied with the remnants of a fading summer suntan. He has a clipboard under his right arm. He stops just short of where I'm sitting and looks down at the clipboard. Then he pulls a pair of reading glasses from his pocket and rests them on his nose to take a quick look at what's written in the file.

My mind immediately goes to a bad place. Something has happened to Henry. Natalie meeting the babies has quickly become an afterthought.

"Hi, Mrs. Rudolph. I'm Dr. Sheppard. I'm here to talk to you about your husband's condition. His surgery went well. We removed a bullet from his shoulder and his abdomen. Now there is some head trauma indicating that a bullet grazed his head, but it didn't impact the brain. And, as you know, we've induced a coma to reduce any swelling in his brain and lower his adrenaline levels." He pauses and clears his throat, then runs his pointer finger down the sheet he's been referencing.

Natalie moves closer and rests her hand on my shoulder.

"Imagine putting your brain on ice," Dr. Sheppard continues. "You want the brain in the most restful state possible to counteract the swelling. If he were awake, he could be agitated and experience immense pain." Dr. Sheppard looks up at me, holding my gaze and willing me to acknowledge that I understand his esoteric prognosis.

"There is a complication, however."

Natalie squeezes my shoulder in anticipation of his answer.

"One of his kidneys is vulnerable due to all of the trauma and is on the verge of failure." He refers to the clipboard again.

"And?" Natalie snaps.

He doesn't seem fazed and proceeds to flip through the notes.

"We'll continue to monitor him for the next thirty-six to seventy-two hours; we'll then be able to determine if a transplant is required. Another determining factor will be if there is a donor available."

Transplant—what is happening here?

"Dr. Sheppard, I'm sorry. Maybe I'm not following. I thought you said his surgery went well. Does this mean he's not getting better?" I can see my query is making Natalie fidget. Her movement mirrors how I'm beginning to feel, but I need to know what happens next.

"So what's the next st—"

Mid-sentence, Natalie cuts me off.

"Seriously, Doc, get the fucking marble out of your mouth and tell us what needs to be done.

What happens if he doesn't get a kidney?"

He shoots Natalie a disapproving look but otherwise maintains his professional demeanor. "As I was saying before the colorful interruption, a kidney transplant would be optimal to assist in his healing. But if that doesn't present as an option, we'll keep him in the coma as long as needed to avoid unnecessary stress on the kidney."

I'm deflated. I don't want to ask any more questions because I can't bear to hear more bad news. With barely a whisper, the words fall from my quivering lips. "How much longer will he be in the coma?"

"I got it!" Natalie shrieks. She grabs Dr. Sheppard by the lapels of his lab coat and pulls him close. "Doc, take my kidney. I only need one, right? This woman is the closest anyone can ever come to having a sister without sharing a womb—I'll give both kidneys if it means she gets her husband back. Now tell me what I need to do."

He gently moves her back to regain his personal space and clears his throat again.

"It's really not that simple, I'm afraid. There are blood and tissue compatibility tests that need to be conducted to determine if you are a match, and also we need to test for antibodies," he lectures.

"But can it be done if I'm not compatible?" she presses.

"Technically, yes."

And before he can continue, Natalie butts in. "Then no further discussion is needed. Let's go do the tests. We have time, right? You just told us he has to stay in the coma anyway."

Dr. Sheppard turns to me. "Izabel, there is a chance that your husband will reject the kidney if the compatibility is less than fifty percent of a half-match. You need to decide if it's worth the risk."

I toggle between the two of them. In what bizarre world did I wake up in this morning that I have to make this decision?

"Natalie, what are you doing?" I fight back the torrent of tears that are threatening to fall. "Do you know what you're suggesting?"

She drops to her knees in front of me. "Jones, listen to me, okay? I've never been so sure of anything before. I could start fires with how I feel about you. You are the love of my life, and if sharing a piece of me brings the love of your life back, then that's all I need to know."

The sterile eggshell-colored walls start to close in on me as I attempt to register what Natalie is saying, the actual meaning of her words. A shimmer of the glowing blue light warming the girls brings me back to the magnitude of the reality being presented to me.

Natalie wipes away my tears and nods, seeking my answer.

I look over at Dr. Sheppard and the nurse for direction, then I return Natalie's nod, but not without trepidation.

"Okay, Doc, it's settled," she says. "Cut me open." Natalie hops to her feet and marches to the door.

With a look of defeat on his face, Dr. Sheppard turns to me one last time. "Izabel, I'll need you to sign some forms on behalf of your husband after we run the required tests."

Natalie is waiting impatiently at the door, tapping the toe of her studded black Frye bootie.

Dr. Sheppard ignores her. "Once we finalize the results, and if we're able to proceed, we can schedule surgery in the next twenty-four hours."

I stand from my chair as the two of them turn to leave.

"Wait, Dr. Sheppard—what about the other man who was admitted with my husband?"

The doctor looks down at his file and flips a page. "Let's see. Mr. Carmichael?"

"Yes, Bo Carmichael. Is he okay?" I ask anxiously and stand to try and take a peek at what it says on that paper on his clipboard.

He shakes his head. "I'm sorry, Mrs. Rudolph. Unfortunately, they were unable to revive him." The doctor terminates the conversation with an apologetic smile and then leaves the room.

I take a step back. The chair behind me hits the backs of my knees and I fall into it. I let out a horrendous gasp of disbelief and drop my head into my hands. I'm sickened by the news, yet malevolent relief floods through me that it was Bo and not Henry. What kind of human being thinks so cruelly towards another? His poor family must be in so much pain. How could I ever begin to try to console this loss for them? I immediately sympathize with Tippy. Losing the twins would have been my demise. The sorrow and emptiness she must feel right now, no mother should be faced with.

My attitude towards my nurse is no longer that of gratitude and patience. Now I'm angry that I've been left in the dark. I need to talk to somebody who can give me answers. I give her a look that could turn her to stone.

"I want someone to tell me what happened to my husband and to Bo!" I shout, knowing full well that this outburst will get me kicked out of the NICU, and I'll probably lose any chance of getting back into Henry's room now, but I don't care.

"Please keep your voice down, Izabel," she orders authoritatively. "I need you to keep calm."

"No, I will not keep my voice down. I want someone to talk to me right now. My ex-husband is dead. My husband is hooked up to machines in an induced coma, and I almost lost not only one baby, but two. And now my best friend has to give up a kidney. So, don't tell me to keep fucking calm." Raging tears stream down my face.

"Izabel, if you would calm down and let me finish . . ." She gives me a castigating look. "Before we came in, I spoke with the officers who were here earlier looking for statements. They would like to speak with you now."

"I don't understand why it took them so long to tell me." I regard her with a tone far less contentious now.

"They tried earlier, but I told them they would have to wait. You experienced a great deal of trauma today. Your mind and body needed a break."

I look everywhere but at her, embarrassed by my petulant outburst.

"I'm sorry for my . . ."

"Izabel, you have every right to be angry. You've been through a lot today." She gives me a gentle, understanding smile. "Come with me. The officers are in the waiting room."

What will be waiting for me there? Do I want to know what happened after Henry left the house last night?

Do I need those horrific images poisoning my brain? Yes, of course I need to know. I will be of no use during our healing if I don't. The nurse and I reach the waiting room, and I see two officers standing by the vending machine. I'm compelled to tidy myself. I straighten my gown on my shoulders and retie my hair back into a twisted bun—not because I am concerned about how I look, but maybe if I appear a bit more presentable, the outcome of the conversation will be different. Maybe they will tell me that there was a case of mistaken identity and Bo is alive. I'm being ridiculous. Even my subconscious is going crazy. The officers notice I have entered the room. They toss their coffees into the trash and turn their somber attention towards me.

I take a deep breath and swallow down the lump in my throat. Nervous perspiration takes over my body as the realization hits. The truth is inevitable. Bo is dead, and Henry is clinging to his life. I'm seconds from finding out why all this happened and what has changed my life forever.

The police officers acknowledge me. "Hello, ma'am, I'm Officer Brandon, and this is Officer Cruz. Thank you for coming down to talk to us." His introduction is stern but sympathetic. He stands tall with his shoulders squared and his arms crossed behind his back. I feel like a fragile porcelain figurine standing next to these two large bodies. Officer Brandon has a dark complexion and a very prominent jawline, and Officer Cruz has a shaved head and a goatee with sprinkles of gray.

"Ma'am," Officer Cruz says and nods, his stance as steady as his colleague's, "we have a few questions for you. Would you be more comfortable if we sit?"

He motions over to the row of chairs. We walk a few steps towards the chairs, and the officers sit across from me.

Officer Brandon takes a little notebook from his shirt pocket and pulls a pencil from the coil spine.

"I just want to know what happened." I struggle to get the words out while my eyes fill with tears.

Officer Brandon offers an understanding nod. "We're still talking to witnesses, but what we are positive of right now is at approximately 10:00 p.m. yesterday evening, two men were involved in an altercation outside of the Round House Pub. The witness who called 911 recalls a group of perpetrators that surrounded the two men, Mr. Rudolph and Mr. Carmichael, and demanded their personal belongings. The two men then handed over their wallets and other personal items on them. The tall, blond gentleman, who has been identified as Mr. Bo Carmichael, proceeded to shout expletives and lunged towards one of the perpetrators, at which point a weapon was drawn and several shots were fired, and Mr. Carmichael fell to the ground."

I gasp at the detailed description and cover my mouth, trying to hold in the bile that's ascending up the back of my throat.

The officer continues to read from his notepad, "Another witness stated that the other man, now identified as Mr. Henry Rudolph . . ." He looks up at me under hooded eyes before he continues. " . . . was seen running over to Mr. Carmichael and leaned over him, at which point several more shots were fired. When emergency services arrived, Mr. Carmichael was deemed deceased and Mr. Rudolph sustained life-threatening injuries."

Officer Brandon's summary of witness accounts is incomprehensible to me. The thought of Henry slumped over Bo's lifeless body is gut wrenching. I spring from my chair and rush to the garbage can next to the vending machine. With one hand on the can supporting my weight and the other clutching my belly, violently I heave, but nothing comes out. I feel the stretch and tear of my incisions with every horrific gag.

Officer Cruz hurries to my side. He gently places his oversized hand on my tiny shoulder for comfort. "Ma'am, I understand how difficult this must be for you."

I slump my chin to my chest and stare at the discarded coffee cups and snack bags at the bottom of the can. I want to crawl in and curl up like the crumpled trash. He looks over at my nurse, who has been standing by this entire time, for her approval. "We just have a couple more questions for you that could help with our investigation," he says as he gently squeezes my shoulder.

I stand straight and let Officer Cruz escort me back to my chair.

"What was your husband's relationship with the deceased?" Officer Brandon asks, looking down at his notepad.

"His name is Bo," I whisper as the tears roll down my face.

"Of course, ma'am." Officer Brandon's response is programmed, yet sensitive.

"Bo is my ex-husband," I answer, refusing to acknowledge him as past tense. He continues to write in his coil-bound pad.

"And what were the two men doing out together?" he continues what now seems like an interrogation.

Now I'm irritated. "What does their relationship have to do with them being shot?"

"Mrs. Rudolph, please trust me when I say I understand what you're experiencing right now, but the more information we can gather, the better we can do our jobs and find the men who did this to your husband and Mr. Carmichael."

I sniffle and wipe my dripping nose with the back of my hand. "Uh, okay. Well, Bo called my cell last night, and Henry answered because I was in the bathtub." My breath is labored and shaky as I recall the night before. "Bo was drunk, so Henry offered to go pick him up. He's been going through a rough time, and Henry is such a good man. He just wants to help people all the time. He doesn't even question when someone asks . . ." I begin to babble.

"And what time did your husband leave to pick up Mr. Carmichael?"

"Why does it matter what time he left? It doesn't change what happened. He shouldn't have left. Why did I let him go?" I release a ferocious shriek and wrap my arms around my body and begin to rock myself back and forth.

The nurse rushes over to me and lifts me into an embrace. "That's enough for now, gentlemen. Mrs. Rudolph needs her rest."

The nurse sits me in a wheelchair. I remain wrapped around myself; anguish, agony, grief spills out of my every pore. The aches in my body are crippling, my joints throbbing. It even feels like my fingernails are tingling.

Emerging from deep in my belly and rising to the back of my throat is a charring reflux causing intermittent heaves. My eyes are getting heavy—I can't fight the exhaustion anymore.

□ □ □

I wake startled. I'm in a dark room now. I must've fallen asleep. No! I need to be awake for Henry and the girls. How long did I sleep for? After blinking a few times, I start to focus on my surroundings. Using the armrests on the bed, I push myself up a little so I'm in a sitting position. I see the soft blue lights of the glowing pods. I must be back in the NICU with the girls. Then I see my nurse standing to the left of me at the other bed, adjusting a drip bag of some sort. That's Henry. I'm back with him. My brain is moving too fast for my body as I try to shimmy to the edge of the bed. I grab my belly and cringe as the pain proves to be too much, crushing my attempt to slide out of bed to get to Henry's bedside.

"Izabel, slow down. You don't want to have to get those sutures done for a second time. It's not a pleasant experience." She gives me an impassive look.

Defeated, I lie back and let out a sigh.

"Do I get to stay here?" I ask.

"Yes, for now, until you are ready to go home. I convinced the administrator putting you in here would free up a recovery room in the maternity ward." She walks over to me and straightens out my blanket and adjusts my pillows.

"Can I see the girls before I get into the bed?" I ask sweetly.

"They're sleeping now. I'll roll them beside your bed, but you need your rest too. They need their mama strong to help them heal."

"Aren't they beautiful?" I say more as a proclamation than a question.

"Don't tell anyone I said this, but they are the cutest ones here." She places her index finger over her pursed lips and grins. "Have you decided on names yet?" she asks with genuine interest.

"I have actually. From the first day I met Henry, he always says everything happens for a reason. That our lives are destined to take a certain path. We just have to decide what its purpose is, that we have to live by choice and not by chance. I don't think I will ever be able to explain why yesterday happened, but I did have a brief moment of clarity and revelation today. It was then when I knew what these babies' names needed to be, and I know Henry will be thrilled that his philosophy on life is the reason." The nurse regards me with wide, curious eyes and a gentle smile.

I put my hand on Babe's belly. "Her name is Hope." And then I rub Little Rudi's belly. "And her name is Faith."

"Well, I think those are wonderful names, Izabel," my nurse says adoringly, and then she turns out the lights and leaves me alone with my family.

8

It's been three days since I dropped to my knees in triage. It's morning again, and I'm pacing back and forth across the room between Henry and the girls. So much has happened. I've struggled a lot with my wavering emotions about life and death. I have a dwelling resentment, but there is now so much to be grateful for. So much to be grateful for, but I have a dwelling resentment that's unsettling. The good news is Natalie was a healthy match for the kidney transplant. Although I didn't want her to back out—selfishly—I did leave the "door" open for her to back out just in case she had any second thoughts about going through with the surgery. She didn't bite, *thank goodness*, and so far so good, Henry's body hasn't rejected it. The doctors are telling me that he's recovering on track and in a couple of days, they should be able to bring him out of the coma. That news flooded me with relief. I felt as if I'd been holding my breath for days and now I can finally breathe again.

I'm able to move around with much more ease now. My sutures are still tender, but they pale in comparison to the pangs I feel every time I look around the room and see the three people I love the most in my life hooked up to machines that are keeping them alive.

"Good morning, Rudolph family," my nurse sing-songs as she throws the door open.

"Good morning, Janet." With the many, many distractions over the last couple of days, we just formally introduced ourselves yesterday when she was changing my bandages. Well, she already knew my name by the countless times she had to tell me to calm down.

"I brought you something that might just bring a smile to your face." She hands me a paper bag that she had tucked behind her back.

The slightest hint of excitement creeps over me as I open the bag and I see the chocolate croissant. I look up at Janet, and she gives me a little wink. I haven't eaten since I've been here, with the exception of a few spoonfuls of applesauce I ate out of protest to avoid the threat of being hooked up to the IV. Mid-chew, I thank her.

"Janet, when do you take a break? You've been run off your feet since I, I mean *we*, got here."

"You're sweet to worry. I take breaks when I need to," she says as she checks one of the wires on the babies in the incubator that has become their temporary home.

"It must be hard to be away from your family for days at a stretch," I say, almost apologizing for monopolizing her time.

She moves from the baby pod over to Henry's bed. "My job right now, my dear, is to make sure you four get healthy and go home. Now finish your breakfast and wash up. We have a busy morning. I'm going to show you some movements you can do for Henry while he heals."

Her invitation to help is revitalizing. I shove the last bite of pastry in my mouth and shuffle over to the sink, scrubbing my hands and face. I take a handful of tap water and gargle audibly. This will be the first intimate interaction with Henry since . . .

Standing next to Henry now is unnerving. My limbs are rigid from my apprehension. The magnitude of what happened to him comes flooding back with force. *What if I hurt him?*

It's as if she read my mind. "You won't hurt him. Your touch will be good for him." Janet wraps her right hand under Henry's knee and gently lifts and bends it about an inch off the bed. She repeats the motion two or three more times. Then she gestures for me to move to the other side of the bed and take my turn. With a feather-light touch, I place my hand on Henry's knee. The usual lightning bolt of energy that's exchanged when we touch is now a void fissure.

"I don't know if I can do this. This isn't Henry."

"You can, Izabel. This is Henry, and he needs your touch." She lifts his leg, then lowers it again. "Wait, I have an idea for you." Janet takes her phone from her pocket and taps in her password. She hands it over to me. "Scroll through my playlist and find a song. I find music always helps." She smiles.

With one hand resting on Henry's leg, I scroll my thumb over the song titles until I stop on Debussy's "Clair de Lune," the romantic piano piece that has traveled through time with us. As the first few soft, melodic notes begin to play, my apprehension is relieved, and I'm swept away for a brief moment, remembering how it all began: my experience with Charlie and Eve, my forever with Henry.

I see Janet sneak out of the room, and I continue on with my touch therapy. First with his legs, then I move down to his ankles and toes, rolling them first clockwise, then the other way. Never taking my hands off his body, I move up to his right side and take his hand into mine. I bring his hand up to my face and caress it down my cheek, stopping on my lips, kissing his palm. *We're going to get through this. I promise.*

The door creaks open. I look up, expecting to see another nurse or doctor, but there standing in the doorway is a sparkle of light that has come to help fight my darkness, and with the most heartwarming whisper, I hear her say, "Hi, my love."

After a few blinks to gain focus, I gently place Henry's hand down by his side and rush over and throw my arms around her and begin to gently weep.

"I'm here now, Izabel. Mommy's here to help you. You're not alone anymore. And next time you convince me to take a vacation, I'll vehemently decline—understood?" She clears my hair from my eyes and wipes my tearstained face. I pout and nod.

We wanted to send Mom on an all-inclusive Jamaican trip to relax for a bit before the baby was born—well, at the time we thought there was only one baby. She's always working and never takes a break, and we wanted to give her a pre-baby gift as a thank you for all the work we knew she was going to do for us.

We walk hand in hand over to Henry's bed.

She caresses his face and leans down to kiss his cheek. Mom then rests her hand over his heart, careful not to interfere with the tubes and tape affixed to him. She looks at me and smiles.

She pats his chest ever so gently and says, "This man's heart is so big and filled with so much love for you, Izabel. It's the only thing that gives his life real meaning. His journey is not over; he'll come back to you." She straightens up her posture and lightly claps her hands. "Now let me see these babies you two made."

Mom peeks a look into the pod and releases a delighted gasp. "Oh, Izabel, they're absolutely beautiful," she proclaims. "Can I touch them?"

I nod yes. "Put your arms through the openings." I watch Mom move with excitement, but slowly, like she's putting a full turkey into the oven, and introduce her soothing strokes to the girls.

"Janet, my nurse, said I'll be doing some skin time with them later. She said they need to feel my body heat and heartbeat and that we can arrange the babies to lie next to Henry, too, so..."

I'm mid-conversation with Mom when Natalie busts through the door. Even in a wheelchair she's her usual "bull in a china shop" fashion. "Jones, can you believe those fuck—"

She stops dead in her tracks when she sees Henry on the bed, with his aggregate of tubes, machines, and wires beeping and clicking. This is the first time she's really seen him in this state with all of the chaos the last few days. Her recovery from the transplant surgery was fairly textbook, but she had to stay in her room and sit still to avoid infection. Despite being cut into, Natalie quite enjoyed being stuck in bed hopped up and hooked up on intravenous opioids. She even tried to charm one of the nurses to shake her up some vodka and pour over ice with a few briny olives. *Let's get this party started*, she kept singing.

She inches her way out of the wheelchair and stands. She winces and extends her arms out, motioning for me to move in closer for a hug.

"Jones, I'm so sorry," she blubbers. "I had no idea—I was so worried about you, and then the whole surgery thing happened—then they were sucking tubes of blood from my arm. To top it all off, can you believe just now the nurses tried to tell me only immediate family could come in." She stops and takes a deep breath.

"Oh my god and the babies!" Nat looks in the pod. "Ew, why are they so wrinkly?" She plants a signature Nat butt slap on me and pulls me in again for another hug.

"I'm just kidding. Jones . . . look, you have babies. Look at them. I've always wanted real-life dolls to dress up."

Right now, I appreciate that she can always make every situation about her. The tension that I've been holding in my shoulders is slowly dissipating, having her by my side now. Like I've always said, I'm the moth to her flame.

"There won't be any dressing up any time soon. They'll be in oversized diapers and dressing gowns for the next few weeks, until I can take them home with me."

"Well, you did evict them before their lease was up. You're a slumlord, Jones." She winks at me, and for the first time in days, I laugh. Even Mom is laughing at Nat's attempt at levity.

"Stop, you're going to make me bust a stitch," I beg.

Mom grabs both Natalie and me by the hand and offers comforting squeezes. "Even miracles take time, girls. We'll all get through this together."

Hearing the sounds of laughter will be good for Henry. It's good for me. Maybe, right now, he's dreaming about everyone he loves hanging around our house, drinking and eating and playing games. His mom organizing a competitive game of charades.

Just as I was beginning to be in the moment and enjoy the banter, the door opens again.

We all look over to see who's come in.

Tippy!

9

I hear the screech of the tires on the driveway. My teeth are chattering, and I can't feel my fingers or toes. There's muted commotion all around me, but I don't respond.

"Not again. How long has she been out here?" I hear Henry ask. His voice is filled with panic. If it wasn't for the tree behind me keeping me perched upright, I would be lying flat on my back, willing the ground to swallow me up. Why do I keep doing this to him? He doesn't deserve to see me like this over and over again. I don't deserve to feel like this. I didn't ask for any of this to happen to me, to us.

"At least three hours. I tried to get her to come inside, but she refused. That's when I called you." Mom sounds overwhelmed and disappointed. Her tolerance for my episodes lately has diminished. The last time this happened, she told me to snap out of it, that I have a family to take care of.

In one fell swoop, I am in Henry's arms. He carries me into the house and up the stairs. He takes me into our bathroom and sits me on the bench under the towel rack. "I'm going to run you a warm bath. Okay, baby?"

Shivering, I wait on the bench and watch the tub fill up. The thick fog that occupies my mind won't clear for a while. Controlling my beast had been much easier over the last few months, but today it caught me off guard.

Fucking Tippy, what was she thinking sending that package over? After the accident, I spent a lot of time with Dr. Kennedy learning how to cope with the fears and anxieties that had developed, going over methods that I had explained and taught my own patients time and time again. But I was not successful practicing what I preached. I was plagued by a hearty combination of post-traumatic stress, postpartum, and survivor's guilt. As well as prescribing SSRIs and SNRIs, Dr. Kennedy suggested I name my beast. He said if I humanize the panic, it would become easier to control. By naming my beast, I was able to legitimize what I was feeling and not let it define who I was. Well, today Keres had the upper hand; she came out of left field and smacked me across the face, knocking me on my ass. In Greek mythology the Keres were spirits of violent and cruel deaths. They were cravers of blood who feasted upon it after ripping a soul free from the mortally wounded. A tad morose, possibly, but certainly fitting for what I was trying to accomplish.

"Stand," he orders delicately. I do as I'm told and let him strip me down. Taking his hand, I steady myself on one leg and dip my toe into the claw-foot tub. The water is hot, probably too hot, but I am chilled to the bone. I step in and sink to the bottom. Holding my breath, I submerge myself under until I completely disappear. After what feels like an eternity, I reluctantly bob my head back up enough that my eyes and nose are above the water. Ashamed that Henry has to treat me like a child, I avoid making eye contact with him. With hooded eyes, I stare down at the still water above my chest.

"Henry, I know what you are going to say. Can we not analyze this right now? I feel worthless as it is. What kind of mother . . ." I pause and sink below the water again. When I pop back up, I blurt, "What kind of mother ignores her babies all afternoon because she is completely removed from reality and can't get her shit together?"

"Izabel—baby, I just want you to be better. When you and Dr. Kennedy decided to wean you off your medication, I completely supported your decision. Only you know your body and what works for you, but maybe it was just too soon. Dr. Kennedy said—"

"You and Dr. Kennedy think you know what it's like to be in my head. Do me a favor. Stop talking to me like you're my therapist, and just be my husband," I hiss.

"I just want to be alone right now. Henry, please leave." The hurt that seeps from his eyes would normally be my undoing, but I'm too irritated from a combination of self-loathing at my inability to gain control and Henry's ability to let everything go. He opens his mouth to respond to my request for isolation but gets up and leaves the bathroom instead.

Left alone to wallow in my mental aberration, I slide down the backrest of the tub, stopping when the water line is just below my eyes, lingering like a starving alligator waiting for its prey. I would gladly offer myself up as bait right now.

□ □ □

An hour later, still hiding out in the bath, trying to avoid facing Henry after being a colossal asshole to him, I can't hold off any longer. I need to apologize. Plus my skin has pruned and is turning a bruised blue. Wrapped in my oversized terrycloth robe, I slink down the hallway towards the girls' bedroom, half hoping Henry will be asleep with them so I can delay the inevitable discussion until tomorrow.

I extend my head in around the doorframe cautiously, but our eyes meet instantly. The girls are asleep on each of his arms, and he's gazing straight ahead. His face is expressionless. Almost as if he's looking right through me. Only I can fix this.

"Hey—remember me? The jackass from the bathroom?" I follow with a pouty lip.

Henry responds with a limp grin. He stands and walks toward the cribs. First, he bends over Hope's crib and lays her on her side. Faith doesn't even move through the downward motion; he has her secured tight against his body. He then lays Faith in her crib and kisses his pinky finger and presses it against her little chin dimple like he does every night. My heart skips a beat, and a little lump grows at the back of my throat as a tear threatens to escape my eye.

Henry walks past me and stops just outside the door. He reaches his hand back and takes my hand into his and weaves his fingers through mine. We walk in silence to our bedroom at the end of the hall. Then we sit at the edge of the bed, shoulder to shoulder, fingers still intertwined, not saying a word. I remain quiet and listen to his calming, rhythmic breaths. I yearn to experience his presence right now. We're on his time.

He'll say something when he's ready. The anticipation is increasing my pulse.

Henry lets go of my hand and turns to face me. "Izabel, you are the love of my life. Me and the girls, well, we don't make sense without you. Do you remember our very first date when I told you about my brother's first wife who died in a car crash and how shitty I felt about having the audacity to enjoy life while he was suffering with his grief?"

I nod yes and then drop my gaze down to the shag area rug under our feet while he continues to talk.

"Izabel, have the audacity. I'm begging you. Let's live our lives . . . let's be happy again. I'm here with you for as long as we're meant to be together, but if you continue to allow the demons to dominate and manipulate your mind, it's going to rob the best pieces of you. The way you nibble on your bottom lip when you're deep in thought and you don't think anyone is looking, the way you can make me laugh like no one else can, and that way you give me the look of desire from across the table, even when you're covered in baby puke and pureed carrots."

Embarrassed, sad, and deflated, finally, I look up at Henry. "I'll do better, and I'll pop in and see Dr. Kennedy next week when I'm back in the office. I promise."

Henry stands up in front of me and extends his arms, gesturing for me to hug him. He holds me close, and we stand flush for a few minutes.

"Come on, Jones. Let's go to bed. Tomorrow's a new day."

10

The weekend was quiet. It was unusual, but a nice change of pace. No family or visitors around, seeing as everyone will be gathering at our house for the holiday. I needed the time with just Henry and the girls. Then I did some shopping for our Thanksgiving dinner that we've hosted every year for the past five years since we got married. Mom usually takes a break and visits friends on weekends, so she wasn't around to help.

I actually had to force her to start taking time for herself on weekends. For the first few months, I would have to pry the girls from her arms if I wanted any time with them. Between Mom and Henry, the only time I was able to hold them was when I was breastfeeding in between pumps. We were told that bottle feeding with breast milk in tandem with breastfeeding would help Henry bond with them better because . . . well, he couldn't do much when they were first born. He never missed a scheduled feeding, though, even when the occupational therapist was there. When he was finally able to come home from the hospital, the therapist came to the house every day for two-hour sessions. As he continued to improve, the therapist would come every other day, and then eventually within a couple of months, he was back to exercising and seeing the therapist twice a week. The doctors credited Henry's positive attitude and determination to recovery.

He walked with a cane for a while to take the pressure off the leg where the bullet hit him, but that didn't last long after Natalie gave him a get-well-soon gift that consisted of a top hat and a monocle and started calling him Mister Peanut. He laughed, but then told her to fuck off and limped away.

The knock on my door snaps me out of my reverie. "Come in."

Dottie pops her head in without opening the door the whole way. "Dr. Jones, your Mr. Smith is here for his double appointment.

I drop my head into my hands. I don't know if I have the energy to deal with him today.

"Oh love, you'll be okay. It's a lang road that's no goat a turnin'," she says and smiles.

I give her an inquisitive look.

"It's just an old Scottish saying. Everything is going to be okay, dolly," she says and shuts the door.

Maybe she should sit with Mr. Smith today. I spent years in school learning how to read people, and with one look and an old Scottish proverb, Dottie has me all figured out.

□ □ □

A mind-numbing two hours later, and I'm back at my desk. Okay, I'm just going to say what I'm not supposed to say, at least not out loud. Sometimes I want to shake

Mr. Smith and tell him that his problems are infinitesimal. His wife asking him to put his towel in the laundry basket instead of on the floor next to it doesn't mean she's secretly plotting against him. I know we all process information differently and that our insecurities are subjective, but come on, man. Just put your fucking towel in the laundry basket—seems pretty simple. *That's so unprofessional Izabel, get a grip—come on.* I smack my notepad on my forehead a couple of times to snap me out of my censuring.

The ping of my cell phone is a welcome diversion for my displaced frustration—another text message from Natalie, the sixth one today. Her timing is quite apropos because she would've let Mr. Smith have it. Professionally, I have to keep my inner Natalie tucked away during my sessions.

She wants me to meet her at 2Kats tonight. I have no desire to be engulfed in the noise of strangers right now. It was our old stomping ground, but we haven't been there in years. I'll respond later. I have time before Henry picks me up if I change my mind.

It's already noon. The wall clock is taunting me with every ticking sound. Henry bought this silly waffle-shaped clock for me from a garage sale when I was pregnant. He thought it was funny because I went through a waffle-craving phase for about a month during my pregnancy. I ate so many that now I can't stand the sight of waffles.

Ticktock, ticktock, the taunting continues. I know I promised Henry I would pop in to see Dr. Kennedy, but I feel good right now and was nightmare-free all weekend. It could be I'm experiencing a bit of a breakthrough, and the thought of evoking demons today is stirring up some anxiety, so in my professional opinion, I do not need to see my therapist today.

My cell phone rings, interrupting my self-assuredness. It's Henry. Come on, it's as if that man has a tracking device on my brain, infiltrating my thoughts.

I let it ring a couple more times before I answer. "Hi, babe."

"Hello, my love. How is your day going?" he asks.

"Oh, you know, just the usual." I never tell Henry about my patients, even Mr. Smith. He also has never asked. He would never put me in the position to break patient confidentiality.

"Are we still on for a five o'clock pickup? I can call your mom and ask her to take some steaks out for us, and I can throw them on the barbeque when we get home."

"Yeah that sounds great . . . Wait. Natalie wants me to meet her at 2Kats, but I haven't answered her yet—not sure I want to, plus you know I don't like sleeping at the condo alone." My answer is wavering.

"You should go, babe. You deserve a night out and a full night's sleep without the babies. Plus, you pumped this morning. I can handle it," Henry proclaims.

"I know, but . . ."

My decision was definitive until Henry cuts me off.

"Hey, did you go see . . ."

I know what he's going to ask before he asks it, so I break in.

"You're right, Henry. I should go see Natalie. She's been staying quiet about Benjamin, so I need to pry it out of her," I pivot.

"Yes. I can't wait to hear more about him too."

He giggles like a gossipy schoolgirl.

I echo his giggle.

"Okay, babe, have fun."

"Thanks. I'll call later to say good night to the girls."

□ □ □

"Well, look what the cat dragged in." Nat gulps down whatever was left in her glass and stands to hug me. "It's just like old times, Jones. I'll get drunk and be flirty, and you'll have to pull me from some bathroom stall and drag me home." She shoots me with fake finger guns.

"Absolutely not, Natalie. We're going to grab a quiet booth, and you're going to tell me what is going on with you and Benjamin," I scold.

"Boo, you're boring, and why do you have those beautiful knockers all wrapped up." She grabs my scarf and unties it from around my neck, then cups my boobs and lifts them, revealing my cleavage.

I playfully slap her hands away. "Stop it, you weirdo."

"Come on, let's get you a drink." She grabs me by the arm and starts dragging me to the bar, pushing through the people waiting to order their drinks.

At some point in the night, the music gets so loud our conversation gets drowned out by the tweaking of the high-pitch treble. The rousing vibration of the deep bass lures us onto the dance floor. The room is spinning, but I'm entranced by the tremor under my feet. Natalie keeps filling my glass to the brim before I have a chance to contest. I wouldn't be surprised if I drank the entire bottle on my own. I vaguely recall a tequila shot or two the countless times she snapped her fingers at the bartender. I feel someone's arms wrap around my waist and mold flush with my body. We start to sway to the music. I take his hands and lift them higher as we continue to move to the beat. Suddenly, I'm being jerked to one side.

I hear Natalie's voice. "Take your fucking hands off her. Can't you see she's drunk? You creep. Get out of here before I smash you in the face." The guy scurries away at Natalie's demand.

I pull my arm away from Natalie. "Hey, I was dancing with him."

"No way, Jones. You're getting messy, and this isn't happening. Let's go." She drags me to the door and down the stairs.

Out on the sidewalk, I release my arm from her clutch. "I'm messy! You think I'm messy?" I point my finger at her, trying to focus my vision by winking one eye closed.

"I've been cleaning up your shit since we were fourteen years old."

"Whatever, Jones." She holds up an extended hand and laughs at me.

"Don't you dare laugh at me. You don't understand. You don't know what's going on." I pound my head with my palms, trying to punch the drunk out of me. "Oh no, what have I done? Henry is so good, and I'm drunk and messy, letting some guy wrap his arms around me," I cry.

"Yeah, you're messy right now, but let's talk about what just happened, Jones. What were you thinking?"

Her response makes me mad. "You got me drunk. It's your fault this happened. You're a garbage panda," I slur.

"Jones, what the fuck are you talking about? You don't even know how to insult someone properly." She laughs harder this time.

"Yes, I . . ." Before I can finish my sentence, I vomit into the concrete planter beside us.

"Okay, party girl, I'll give you a pass on this one." She concedes and hails us a cab.

11

Why do hangovers get worse the older you get? It's been two days, and I still feel like crap. Thank god for mom, or I wouldn't have been able to get anything done for dinner today. I rub my pulsing temples. The conversations around the table might as well be a heavy metal band playing next to my head. What are they all laughing at? They think it's easy having ten-month-old twins and preparing Thanksgiving dinner for twenty people. The back and forth banter of one-liners and bad jokes is becoming unbearable.

Why did the cranberries turn red? Because they saw the turkey dressing.
Why can't you take a turkey to church? Because they use FOWL language.
The turkey's been in the oven for hours, and it's still running around.

Laughter erupts in the room again. Perspiration is starting to drip from my armpits. The feeling of spider legs crawling up my back is getting more intense, and the walls start to close in on me. I grab my plate and walk over to the sink. I take a deep breath, and then I slam the plate down, busting it into pieces. Slivers of my wedding china slide across the countertop.

Then there's silence. Everyone stops their chatter and looks over at me. "Now that I have your attention, do you all think that's funny? Anyone else have a joke about my turkey?"

Henry goes to stand up to come to me and Natalie grabs his arm. I hear her say, "No, I'll go."

Like a bear to his honey, Natalie is by my side at the sink and grabs my arm. She whispers in my ear. "Let's go upstairs."

With one arm securely tucked under Natalie's, I manage to snatch the extra poured glass of wine from the counter with my free hand before she pulls me in the direction of the stairs. Without acknowledging my guests or Henry, Nat and I walk past them, down the hall and up towards the master suite. She doesn't let me out of her clutch.

Behind closed doors and in the confinement of my bedroom, Natalie releases me.

"Dude! What was that all about? You know I love a good Britney meltdown as much as the next person, but you could never pull off the shaved head. That was kind of embarrassing." She laughs it off.

"It's not funny, Natalie. You can't joke your way out of everything. Some of us have real shit going on in our lives."

"I don't think it's funny, Jones. Honestly. I'm just worried about you—and Henry. And the girls need you. You can't lock yourself up in your room any time something doesn't go your way. That's really selfish."

She moves in closer to smack my butt.

I pivot to avoid her contact.

"Are you fucking kidding me right now? What the hell would you know about family?" I shout and gesture dramatically with my hands.

Her eyes widen.

"Don't you even dare throw your self-righteous bullshit at me."

Ignoring the massive hangover migraine drilling a hole into my left temple, I chug the remaining Petite Sirah from the glass that I've been flailing around, staining my white faux sheepskin throw rug.

"Nobody can erase what happened. You will never be able to experience the torment that destroyed my mind, my entire existence that day."

I see her nod, but she avoids looking at me.

"I'm half dead—because you were able to help him when I wasn't. Do you know how that makes me feel?"

Natalie tries to get a word in, but I keep going.

"You've spent your entire life avoiding commitment, not giving a shit what people think about you or who you hurt along the way, and—and now you are up here trying to tell me what's good for me and my family—ha. You think you know what you're talking about now because you've had a boyfriend for—what?—a minute? I'm sure you will find a way to screw things up with Benjamin just like you have with all of your relationships. You're a screw-up. Do you hear me?"

Seething with bitter hostility, I begin to grab items of clothing from my closet that look like they might have been gifted by Natalie and throw them in a pile on the floor.

"You think because you gave Henry a kidney, you know what's best for him? Did you fuck him too?"

She remains silent and stares at me with a look of disbelief.

"You and Henry think it's so easy for everything to be normal again. Well, guess what? It's not."

I toss a thin-strapped sequin top on the pile.

"Wow. I'm sorry you feel that way." Natalie walks to the door, but pauses and turns to me.

In that moment, I wanted to apologize, but I am struck with silence, disbelief, and shame. How can I begin to excuse the hurtful words that spit from my mouth like venom from a snake on the defense?

"I stand corrected. You do know how to throw an insult. Never in a million years would I have imagined the first time I got my heart broken would be by you." Her eyes swell; she wipes the tears from her eyes and shuts the door behind her.

I jump onto my bed and curl into the body ball that has served as the escape from reality, my portal, and pull the duvet over my head. Then I succumb to the perpetual darkness.

□ □ □

The clock on the bedside table is flashing 7:00 p.m., and the room is black. *How long have I been asleep?* The room lights up when the door to the bedroom opens. Henry walks in and turns on the lights.

"Heyyy." I wince as I'm blinded by the brightness.

"The power went out," he says.

"What time is it?" I ask, flopping back down onto my pillow.

"It's midnight," he answers curtly.

"Why are you coming to bed so late? Did the girls go down okay?" I ask, a little uninterested.

"I had a couple of whiskeys," Henry answers, not hiding the irritation in his tone.

"What's your problem?" I snort.

He gruffs at me and lifts his T-shirt over his head.

"What's wrong with me? Did you go talk to Dr. Kennedy like I asked you to?"

Before I can answer, he begins to unleash on me. "Seriously, Jones, what the fuck? You make a scene at dinner and freak out because of some stupid jokes about the turkey. Then you storm upstairs and hide in our bedroom like a disobedient child." Henry chucks his shirt into the laundry basket and starts pacing the room.

I sit up and look at him. "Henry, I don't really want to have this conversation right now, and you're kind of being an asshole. You don't know what—"

"Izabel, shut up for once in your life and listen!" he shouts. The anger in his voice is apparent. "Stop telling me I don't know what you're going through. I went through it. Remember? I was the one who was shot. I was the one who was in a coma, clinging to life, and I was the one . . ." He stops pacing. "I was the one who watched Bo die right in front of me, leaning over his lifeless body and begging him to hold on. Telling him how important he is to everyone, that he can't die on us." His anger seems to subside and is replaced by grief.

"Do you have any idea how many times I've pulled over on the side of the road to cry and watch image after image flash before my eyes? No, you wouldn't.

Should I have talked to you about it more? Sure, but I was always so concerned about how you were dealing with everything that I pushed all my shit deep down and hid it away."

I'm about to respond, but he holds his hand up to indicate that he's not finished.

"It would have been so easy for me to curl up into a ball and disappear too."

That was a direct jab at me.

"But I didn't have the luxury to wallow in the *what-ifs*. Nor did I want to. I was blessed to have my family by my side. We brought these two beautiful humans into this world, and my main job in life from that moment on was to make sure they're always safe."

"What are you saying? You don't think I'm a good mother?"

Henry plops down on the edge of the bed and drops his head into his hands. "Oh come on, Izabel. You know that's not what I'm saying."

"First Natalie, now you. If you both think I'm doing such a terrible job, why don't I just leave, and the two of you can play happy house. Then you two can actually do it. I see the way you look at her and joke with her."

"Wow—what the fuck? You know what? I'm done with this. Clearly you're not going to listen. My intention wasn't to come in here and fight with you. It was to tell you that I have to go to New York to check in on a project, but I think I'll stay for a while. We need a time-out. I'll visit my parents for a few days."

I can only offer a blank stare.

Henry shakes his head at me. He stands, pauses for a few seconds, and then walks out of the bedroom.

□ □ □

Henry is gone before I wake up. This is the first time in our relationship he's left without saying goodbye. The break might be good for both of us. I fetch the girls from the cribs, and we make our way to the kitchen for another morning of pureed squash, or is it pumpkin? I know it's leftover from Thanksgiving though. What does it matter? Most of it will end up on the floor. I'm in a trance, watching the blender mash its contents. Maybe I should stick my head in there to feel something other than this plague that runs through me.

I'm brought back to reality when I hear Mom singing one of her ceremonial breakfast songs that she made up. "Two for you and one for me—two of you plus me is three." I ignore her and her chipper mood and walk over to the highchairs to help Mom strap the girls in.

"Henry will be out of town for the next few days. Just thought you should know."

Unfazed by my sullen mood, Mom continues to hum her song and hands me a bib for Hope. "Yes, I know. He told me last night."

I huff at her. "What? When?"

"When you were up in bed ignoring your family, Izabel. Henry and I enjoyed a whiskey, and we had a nice chat."

Great, her too. As annoyed as I am with Mom's dig at me, I don't have the energy to have my third fight in twelve hours. I sit in my chair facing the girls and grab the bowls to start feeding the babies. They're both extra fussy this morning. Faith is trying to grab the spoon from my hand, but I divert and fill her mouth with a generous amount of puree. Hope tugs at the bowl, and before I know it, her fingers are swimming in pumpkin.

I look back to Faith, and she's heaving her food down her bib.

"That's it. I've had enough." I stand up so quickly the backs of my legs knock the chair over. The girls start to cry. I walk around the other side of the kitchen island and toss the bowl into the sink.

Mom rushes to the girls to comfort them. "Now look what you've done." She casts me a disapproving scowl. "Izabel, enough of this moping around. You are the most beautiful woman I know, but lately I've never met an uglier person, and I don't mean your looks. Aren't you tired of being angry?"

"Mom, please—I don't need one of your lectures right now, okay?" I roll my eyes and grab some paper towel off the roll to wipe away the puree on my hands.

"Well, I'm sorry, darling. I'm going to tell you something, whether you want to hear it or not. Now come over here and sit down. You're going to listen to me."

Grimacing at her orders, I toss the paper towel into the garbage and sit at the island stool to appease her.

"I'm sitting. What do you need to tell me?" Knowing my mother, it's taking all of her strength not to counterattack the unnecessary attitude I'm casting her way. I'm sure if the girls were sleeping in a different room, she would let me have it.

"Do you remember what you said to me when the girls first came home?"

I respond with a blank stare, partially because I don't remember and partially because I'm being petulant.

She continues, "We were standing over the crib, watching them sleep. You were so overcome with joy and bewilderment at these two beautiful humans that you and Henry created." Mom drapes her hands over mine. A sense of calm runs through me.

"What did you say to me?" Her look is telepathic as she urges me to answer.

"I said it's amazing how instantly I fell in love with them and that I would do whatever I had to do to keep them safe and take away their pain so they wouldn't have to feel any of it." I sigh.

"That hasn't changed, Mom. You're not in my head. It's like every day when I leave my room, I walk into a toxic fog that devours my mind and takes me back to that day. You don't understand." I pull my hands from hers.

"Please stop saying I don't understand. You're my baby, and I want to keep you safe and take all of your pain from you, but you have to let me help. Izabel, you have a storybook life here. A wonderful, loving, and patient husband who's put you on such a high pedestal that you were bound to fall off one day. How long do you expect him to understand though? It would crush me if you stepped out of your fog one day and he was no longer there for you." She closes our distance and hugs me close, but I don't reciprocate at first. Her words have cut me deep. I almost lost him once because of circumstances beyond my control. The thought of losing him again because of something I caused would kill me. I wrap my arms around her and begin to sob, a potent, cathartic release.

"Oh, Mom, I would die if Henry weren't in my life."

She unravels herself from my clutches and looks me in the eyes. "But he is, darling. You haven't lost him.

You and the girls mean the world to him, but you have to let the past go. Live for these beautiful girls." Mom takes a pause to kiss them on the head. "Live for your husband, but most importantly, live for you." She moves closer to the girls and begins to clean them up, removing their bibs and wiping their orange-stained faces.

"Izabel, just remember sparrows always find their way home." She winks at me.

And with Mom's simply profound cliché, I know what I need to do.

12

The street looks exactly how I remember it. The time-chiseled Zelkova trees look as if they've seen their last bloom, bare of leaves with snapping branches as they prepare for the winter months. I walk up the front path with hesitation. *What am I doing here?* I take a deep breath before pressing down on the intercom button a couple of times. The door buzzes open. I slink down the hall, following the distinct, familiar aroma of patchouli, evoking memories of my first regression six years ago. Memories of Eve and Charlie and their undeniable love for each other and how it has single-handedly impacted my life. Before I have a chance to knock, the door creaks open.

"Welcome back, Izabel," Rachel Kimble greets me with a namaste bow. "Please come in and make yourself comfortable." *How will this help Henry and me?*

I walk farther into the room and examine the surroundings, taking inventory of the theological diversity just as I did the first time I was here. Praying Buddha statues, ornate icons of the Virgin Mary, and so many more. I'm nervous yet excited. I'm not sure what I'm expecting to gain from this session.

"Izabel, let's sit." Rachel waves her hand toward the plush seats over by the front window, where we sat last time I visited so many years ago. We sit in silence, but it's not uncomfortable. As I sink into the chair, my shoulders relax, and I'm met with calm. Maybe it's Rachel's energy, or maybe it's because this is where it all started.

"So, Izabel," Rachel begins, "why don't we start slow. Tell me how has your journey been since we last met."

She is so removed from my story that for the first time in months, the burden that comes along with talking about the tragedy is removed. These are just words that she'll be hearing for the first time. There will be no preconceived notion on how I'm supposed to feel and no judgment on how I actually feel.

For the next hour, I talk and Rachel listens. Occasionally she nods and offers a sympathetic look, but she doesn't interject. I tell her about my nightmares, and I recount the tragic week in the hospital, almost losing Henry and the girls, the months of rehab that Henry, that we all, had to endure when he got home.

I take a long pause. The absolute magnitude of saying it out loud again is exhausting. I release a weighty sigh. I continue to tell her about Bo's death and how horrific I feel that I'm relieved it was him and not Henry, that now I live in a fog that has beguiled me so savagely I can't escape, no matter how positive the future looks.

Rachel releases a silent sigh, as if she'd been holding her breath the entire time. "Before we begin, I'd like to offer my deepest apologies and sympathy for what you and your family have had to experience. However, my dear, my offering of regret won't help you heal. How can I assist in your healing process?"

"I don't know actually. I don't know how to snap out of this crippling haze I'm lost in. I thought maybe if I'm removed from my reality and I regress back to when I was thrown into the world of Eve and Charlie, to maybe experience their love story again, it might offer an awaking of my present with Henry and how we were destined to be together."

"I'm afraid that's not possible, dear. That path no longer exists. That story has been told, and it can't be revisited. Your answers aren't in the past; they're in your future."

I drop my head in my hands, feeling somewhat defeated. This was my last resort.

"Izabel, let's talk about your nightmares. Let's release your memories and find your trigger and then free your mind of the demons. What is the last image you see in your nightmares?"

My clarity has never been clearer. There it is—it was staring me in the face the entire time. Tippy is my trigger.

I'm flooded with relief. "Bo's mother is my trigger. She's the last face I see in my nightmares."

"This is good progress, Izabel. I'm not going to put you in a regression state, however; I want you to take me back to the last thing you remember. The frailty of one's subconscious is subjective. We all deal with trauma differently. Now close your eyes, take a few deep, steady breaths, and bring all recollections and awareness to the forefront of your mind."

I follow Rachel's instructions and take slow, deep breaths—*inhale—exhale—inhale—exhale*—until I see Tippy standing in the doorway of Henry's hospital room.

◻ ◻ ◻

Tippy's face looks tired and tearstained; there are faint smudges of mascara under her puffy red eyes. Her usual petite figure is shrunken, although she's still dressed as immaculately as ever. My heart drops to the pit of my stomach. My instinct is to run to her and wrap my arms around her and share her pain, but I can't move. The floor has turned to quicksand, and with every attempt to move, I sink deeper into the void.

I hear her whisper of a voice. "Hello, Izabel."

I'm speechless. I feel Mom brush past me. There is no hesitation to her intentions. Tippy is shadowed by Mom's embrace. Then her diminutive figure disappears behind Mom. Their faint sobs are almost deafening. Even during this horror, Tippy won't let go of her composure.

I hear Mom say, "I wish I could take your pain away. Anything you need, I'm here for you."

Mom motions to Natalie to leave the room with her. Natalie continues to stare at Tippy.

Mom snaps her fingers at her now. Nat jumps and scurries across the room. She gently rests her hand on Tippy's shoulder before she leaves.

We're alone now, forced to confront our destinies. She walks to the end of Henry's bed, grabs the rails, and begins to weep.

"Oh, Izabel, I'm so sorry. This is all Bo's fault."

I rush to her side and hug her. "No—no, Tippy, don't say that."

I let her cry into my embrace. Her tiny shoulders tremble with every breath.

Tippy releases herself from my grip and holds me at arm's length and inspects me up and down.

"Izabel, you look disastrous, darling. Let me have Damien bring you a jumpsuit and some face cream," she deflects.

I want to tell her it's okay to be sad and mourn her son, but who am I to tell her how she should grieve? Instead, I decide only to decline her offer.

"Now show me these babies of yours." She takes my hand into hers and we walk over to the pod. Tippy, without pause, places her arms through the holes, and she begins to stroke the girls with the backs of her hands. A smile replaces the pained expression that she had since she walked into the room.

"What are their names?"

"On your right is Hope, and to the left is Faith."

"Of course. That's absolutely perfect." She begins to hum softly and sway.

I back away and allow her to enjoy this maternal moment that she was quite possibly craving, maybe for years.

Mom and Natalie are back now. The three of them huddle around the babies, and I see mostly smiles with the occasional frown, but I'm not paying attention to what they're discussing. I begin Henry's exercises. I massage up his legs, bending him at the knees and then straightening them again. In my usual pattern,

I move around to the left side of the bed and take his hand into mine so I can roll his wrists.

When I finish up, I interrupt the conversation that's going on around the babies. "It's skin time," I say.

The three of them look at me confused as I roll the pod next to Henry's bed.

"It's something the nurse taught me to do. It's good for Henry and the girls. It helps them bond." They don't question my movements; instead, they watch as I gently pick up each tiny body and place them face down on Henry's exposed chest. Their little bodies rise and fall with Henry's every manufactured breath. The first time I watched the nurse do it, I was mortified. The sight of the three of them with tubes and wires all intertwined was heartbreaking. But when I saw how peaceful they looked lying together, all I wanted to do was to crawl in next to Henry and live his experience.

I hold them in place by their little diapers. They look like two feathers that have fallen off a dove compared to Henry's dark, olive skin.

The trio in the corner release a small fit of laughter, distracting me from my duty.

I feel his weak squeeze around my fingers not once, but twice. I look down. He is awake and smiling at me with his eyes.

"Henry."

□ □ □

Suddenly it dawns on me, my revelation is unmistakable.

"That's it. I've had it wrong this entire time."

"Welcome back, Izabel." I'm received by Rachel's kind, rose-colored face.

"Tippy was never my trigger. For years Tippy was anchored to so much of my unhappiness when I was with Bo that she was the easiest one to blame for all of the negativity that I allowed to take me hostage emotionally over the last year. She was there when Henry woke up. Thank you. Thank you, Rachel. You've made me see things so clearly. I've been punishing myself for months. What I lost wasn't lost at all. I just didn't know where to find it." My voice drifts off as I suddenly remember that Henry and I are in a time-out.

"Izabel, there is no thanks needed. Your answers were going to be clear when you were ready to see the truth. I'm here to listen. It's my experience that answers can be found in the questions you have. You just have to know how to ask them."

"Now I need to mend my marriage. I have a lot of apologizing to do to Henry—to everyone."

"Izabel, sparrows always find their way home."

"What did you just say? My mom just said the same thing to me the other day."

"Well, your mother is a very wise woman."

"Yes, she is."

13

My sleep was restful and nightmare-free. It takes me a few seconds to realize that Henry is not in bed with me. For the first time in months, his absence doesn't trigger fear. I encompass an incredible sense of calm. Today I let go of the pain. Today I exhume my disembodied presence. My precious girls need their mother back, my husband deserves the life he chose—and I need to get my Natalie back. There have been so many times in our lives when I've been so irate, so irritated, and even vowed to never speak to her again.

I laugh as I remember our last big fight. Henry and I had just reunited, and she and Portia had pseudo ended a few weeks earlier. He was still living in New York; we would go a week or two without seeing each other. It was torturous. When he would come to Chicago to visit for a few days, she would find a way to infiltrate or sabotage our time together and spend the entire time asking about Portia. Now, looking back, I know she wasn't doing it on purpose, but at the time, I was so angry with her. I wanted Henry all to myself and to spend every minute together like new couples do. She took the breakup with Portia harder than she would admit.

I guess hanging out with Henry was her way of being close to Portia without giving anything away. One day I finally had to tell her to butt out and get her own life. It was hurtful at the time, but that only lasted a couple of days before she was back in our condo tucked between Henry and me in bed, marathoning Netflix shows.

But this time, my outburst was so hostile, so hurtful. She has never ignored my calls before. I have to be delicate with her. She didn't deserve my unprovoked wrath. I dial her number again and cross my fingers in hopes she answers this time. Her accepting my apology is pivotal to my healing process. The thought of her not being in my life is ... no, I can't think that way. We're bonded. We have shared and lost so much of our life together.

After six rings, I hear her voicemail. It is eight in the morning. I don't think Natalie has been awake before nine ever in her life, but I had to try. Plus, if she did answer, chances are I've awakened her and she'll be disoriented and have no choice but to listen to me. She'd agree to anything if it meant she could go back to sleep. I need to see her tonight, though, and make things right before Henry comes home. He's scheduled to come back in a couple of days, and I want to be able to concentrate on him once he's back. He hasn't been completely radio silent; there was constant checking in on the girls, but not much else. How can I blame him? My behavior has been horrendous over the last few weeks.

I can hear sounds coming from the girls' room. It's time to get up and get the day started. Their babbling baby conversation gets louder the closer I get to their room, and it's making me smile. It feels so good to smile again. When I walk into the room, I find the girls leaning over their cribs, giggling and babbling over each other.

"Sounds pretty important, girls," I say, laughing at them. They look at me and start jumping around like little monkeys. I lift Faith first, and then Hope, then we begin our morning routine. The routine I've been emotionally void from. How I've missed this. I grab them both and squeeze them tight and blow raspberry kisses all over them. They erupt with excitement.

"What are you three making so much noise for?" I hear my mom say as she stands in the doorway.

I tickle them more. "Girls, look! Nana's here! Nana's here!"

"Somebody's in a good mood this morning," Mom chimes.

"You're right. I am in a good mood. I know what I need to do now, Mom, and I'm going to start with Natalie," I announce and smile.

"I'm proud of you, Izabel. I knew you'd find your way back. Do you need my help?"

I examine her kind, soft face; she is genuine to the core. I only hope I can live up to her caliber of motherhood.

"I love you, Mom," I declare.

"I love you, too, darling. Now go shower and get out of here and go to her. You have some making up to do."

I hop to my feet and almost crush Mom with my hug.

"Okay, let's take the girls downstairs, and then I'm going to shower. Can you feed the girls for me?"

Mom gives me a look of amusement. We scoop them up and head downstairs for some oatmeal and applesauce.

□ □ □

The drive into the city gave me a lot of time to compose what I was going to say to Natalie. If she won't answer my calls, then I'll have to ambush her. It's Sunday. She doesn't go anywhere on Sunday unless it's for a social brunch and there are mimosas and . . . actually just mimosas.

After I park, I walk over to the coffee shop and get Natalie's favorite, a double espresso with steamed coconut milk. This is my attempt at extending an olive branch—the whole olive tree, really.

The ambush is working in my favor. I don't have to buzz up to Natalie. Someone was walking out as I approached the door. Watching the elevator count down the floors to the lobby was torturous. It would be so easy to run away so I don't have to face her and wish none of this happened.

The door to her condo might as well be a brick wall. I may have to chip away at it slowly so it doesn't crumble to the floor. I rap dubiously on the door, my knuckles barely touching the cold steel surface. The feeling in the pit of my stomach is that of dead butterflies. I take a deep breath and wait for her to answer. The door swings open and Natalie is standing in front of me with a big, welcoming smile, and then she deflates with disapproval.

"Nope." She shakes her head and slams the door.

I place my fingers on the door in regret. The metal barrier that separates us couldn't feel colder.

"Natalie, please, we need to talk. And I have your favorite coffee and a cream cheese muffin," I add, hoping to lighten the mood.

She opens the door again, ever so slightly grabs the coffee and the muffin-filled bag, and then she is gone again.

I contemplate walking away, but I can't risk losing her forever. Natalie needs to hear what I have to say. My body slides down the wall until I'm perched on the floor. I rest my back against the door for support. I have a feeling I'll be here for a while. I'll stay as long as it takes.

Where do I start? I click my nails along the door a few times. "I understand you don't want to let me in, but please just listen to what I have to say, and then I'll leave, and you'll never have to see me again if you don't want to. I love you so much that if not seeing me ever again is what will make you happy, then that's what I'll do."

I take a deep breath through my nose, hold it for a few seconds, and then release it through pursed lips. Okay, let's begin.

"Do you know how proud I am of you?" I pause, hoping for a response, but I know I'll literally just be talking to the door. "Of course you don't because I've never told you. Our relationship from the beginning has always been this symbiotic connection where you get in trouble and I bail you out, but I've come to realize that wasn't the case at all. I martyred myself, thinking that you always needed saving, that that was the purpose in my life. The truth is it was me who needed saving. From the day we met, you were always so confident with who you are. You dressed for you, regardless of what other girls would say. If your hairstyle started to look too mainstream, you would dye it some outrageous color or completely shave it off without a care.

By the time we were fourteen, you made it perfectly clear to everyone that your love was fluid, that you were going to love who you wanted, when you wanted. Even with all the backlash and name-calling from the students, you still set up an anonymous hotline at your house for anyone to call who was struggling with their identity and didn't have anyone else to talk to—and you always defended the underdog, and still do to this day. What did I do? I stayed quiet because I was afraid the popular group that I desperately craved attention from wouldn't like me."

Natalie used to call that group the Heathers, from a movie that was before our time, but Nat said *Heathers* was the original *Mean Girls*.

"I remember that one day in tenth grade when I showed up at your place, crying because the Heathers were having a waist-measuring competition, and they started to make fun of me because I was bigger than all of them, and you said to me . . ."

"I said fuck those privileged closet lesbians," Nat interjects, and I hear the anger in her response.

We stay silent for a few minutes. I want to give her the opportunity to say more, but she doesn't.

"Natalie, I said some terrible things that I can't take back. If I could rewind the clock to that moment,

I don't know if I would do anything differently. I needed to hit my all-time low in order to crawl out of the purgatory I was swirling around in and want to heal. See, again, it's you saving me. The fear of that day consumed me, and nothing you or Mom or even Henry would say could alter my hopeless perspective. Some days I didn't even want to see the girls because it was too painful. Even their toothless little grins couldn't resurrect an ounce of tranquility from me.

It was like with every step I took, it felt as if I was walking to the edge of a cliff. I fell off that cliff every day and would have to relive that anguish over and over again. My nightmares haunted me, even when my eyes were open. I can't change it, and I can't excuse it. This is the burden of PTSD with an added sprinkle of postpartum. But you need to believe me when I say"— I take another deep breath and exhale slowly—"I'm sorry for every time I doubted you. I'm sorry for always putting your feelings after my own. I'm just . . . sorry."

More silence passes and still no reaction. Sliding back up the door feels like I'm rising from the dead. Then there's suddenly weightlessness behind me, and I fall flat on my ass into Natalie's entryway.

As I'm lying on her floor covered in my coffee, she looks down onto me. "Well, get up. You have some more groveling to do." She winks and extends her hand to help me stand.

She pulls me into an embrace. Natalie's hold dominates mine, and her grip on me gets tighter, like a python paralyzing its prey.

"Um, Nat, I can't breathe."

She releases me from her clutch and holds me by my shoulders. "Good. Now you know how you made me feel. Like someone had squeezed every last bit of breath out of my lungs and stomped all over it."

Her dramatic portrayal is not lost on me. I drop my head as a sign of penance.

"Jones, I don't make sense without you. I have no desire to live in a life without you in it, but if you talk to me like that again, I'll kick your fucking ass."

She follows with the sweet sound of her laughter. The treble from her laugh reverberates through the deepest cell of my body, instantly evoking peace and delight in me.

"Natalie, I have to—"

"No more," she interrupts. "Trust me when I say we're good. You've been through shit nobody should have to go through. You've recognized and apologized; now we're moving on—like we always do. Now come give mama a real hug."

She pulls me in again and squeezes my butt cheeks. I melt into her and accept her absolute forgiveness.

"Hey, will you help me with something before we go for lunch?" I inquire with a stealthy smile.

"Well, I was supposed to go to lunch with Ben, but this adventure sounds way more fun."

"No, no, don't ruin your plans with Ben," I implore.

She ignores me and clicks away on her phone. "Already done. Let me throw something more presentable on and we'll go."

"Wait, was he on his way here?" I dread to think of how he must feel by her abrupt cancellation.

"Yeah, so? I told him to turn around and go back home," she says without any reservation and skips into her bedroom.

Although her callous response isn't surprising, I still feel terrible for Ben.

She emerges from her bedroom three minutes later wearing a slouchy hat, a multicolored kimono-style jacket, and oversized tie-dyed sweatpants.

I look her up and down. "That's what you're going with?"

Natalie inspects her outfit. "Yeah, why?"

She's like a child who's just been given permission to pick out her own clothes for the first time.

"What the frock, Nat?" I laugh and snort through my nose.

"Uh no—don't even with the bad mom jokes, Jones."

It doesn't matter what she puts on, Natalie always looks runway ready.

14

An hour later, I'm sitting in the swivel chair in front of the ornate oval mirror, waiting for Vince to tend to me. Vince is the most fantastical human being I've ever met. He has the most ridiculous mullet haircut that looks amazing on him. His outfit of choice usually consists of a long, flowy skirt and a vintage rock band T-shirt, and he always sings the sentences in his conversation that he's excited about like a Christina Aguilera riff.

"Izabel, do you know how many years I've waited for you to do this?" He squeals with excitement.

I toss my head from side to side and watch my mousey blond, mid-back-length hair brush back and forth. I'm anxious about my decision, but it's an important decision. It's a necessary molting process. He stands behind me and drapes the cape around me.

"So, are you ready for the new you?" he sings and pulls my hair back into a loose tie for the first cut.

The new me—how apropos? "Yes, let's do this!"

Vince pulls his shears from his back pocket and starts to snip at the air as a dramatic prelude to the big hair chop-off.

"Wait!" Natalie barks. "Let me do it."

Vince examines me, looking for permission. I roll my eyes and nod yes. He hands Natalie the scissors. Her face beams with joy, you would think he just handed her a brick of gold.

Vince turns me away from the mirror. "Okay, ladies, let the transformation begin." He throws his head back and cackles like he's a mad scientist.

Natalie gives him a miffed look and snips my hair just below the tie.

For the next two hours, we gossip about insignificant celebrity feuds, hookups, and breakups. It's mind numbing, and I'm loving every syllable of it. Vince tells us about his new boyfriend, Daniel, and how he thinks *this is the one*. My hair is now rinsed, treated with some avocado oil, and toned. Vince sits me back at his station and places his hands around the crown towel he has wrapped around my head.

"Are you ready, gorgeous?" he sings again.

"I've never been more ready." I can see Natalie in the mirror standing behind Vince, clapping with excitement.

Vince unfolds the towel, and platinum blond strands fall just above my shoulders. My eyes meet Nat's, and she smiles and winks at me.

"Now the fun begins," Vince announces.

"You two finish up, and I'm going to get a table at Lula's. Jones, meet me there."

I acknowledge. Vince continues with a few snips and chops until I see the look of satisfaction on his face. He pulls the blow-dryer from the holster and stands like he's getting ready for an old Western standoff.

With the roller brush in one hand and the dryer in the other, he comes at me to finish the job.

Vince drags his fingers through the messy beach wave and dusts off a few stray hairs.

He pulls the cape from my shoulders. "Et voilà. I am the blond queen—you're welcome," Vince says, admiring his work, fixing a wave or two by twisting them between his fingers.

I rise from my chair like a phoenix from the ashes. My shoulders are cocked back and my chin is high. I look in the mirror, first to the right then the left. I shake the waves back and forth.

"Vince, I love it. You did an incredible job. I don't even recognize myself." A tear escapes and rolls down my cheek.

"Girl, don't you even dare, because then I'll start crying, and I'll have to reapply my mascara," Vince warns.

I rub the moisture off my face. "What do I owe you?"

He smiles at me. "This one's on me, sweetie. You go get him, girl."

□ □ □

Lula's is only a couple of city blocks away, but I'm rushing because Natalie sent me a text to hurry the F up.

I walk in and scan the room, and I see her right away. How can I not by her technicolored outfit? She spots me and stands to her feet. She starts clapping a slow clap and shouts to the entire restaurant: "Excuse me, everyone! Can you all stop what you're doing for a minute and take a look at how beautiful my girl looks?"

Everyone in the restaurant is staring at me now. I'm absolutely mortified. I rush to the table with my head down, trying to avoid eye contact with the other guests. A few diners chuckle but don't seem fazed by Natalie's interruption.

"Natalie, what are you doing?" I scold.

"Are you kidding me, Jones? This look deserves a standing ovation. I can't believe it took your husband almost dying for you to finally do what I've been telling you to do for years."

"Nice to see you're back at it, Natalie. Now can you sit down and stop embarrassing me?"

She finally sits down and hands me the glass of Prosecco she pre-ordered for me.

"A toast," she says, "to healing, to your new life, to the new Jones."

I'm touched by Natalie's tender sentiment.

". . . and to Henry banging you into next week when he lays his eyes on you."

Well, it was nice while it lasted. We clink glasses and take a long sip of the cold bubbles.

"So, when does Henry come back?" she asks between sips.

"Hopefully tomorrow night, but in one of his texts to me, he suggested he might just go straight to work Tuesday morning. I've been so horrible to him, I'm surprised he even wants to come back at all."

"Don't be ridiculous. That man would run through blazing buildings for you and those babies. He's hurt, Jones, but it doesn't mean he doesn't love you. Open your heart and let him in. Let him feel the pain you've been carrying around so he can help you let it go.

You need to do this together."

Behind all of her hard exterior, Natalie does have a bleeding heart.

"I hope you're right."

"Jones, I'm always right. Enough about you for a minute, I have something to tell you."

Before I can respond, the waitress is at our table to take our order.

"Have you had a chance to look at the menu?" she asks.

Natalie cuts in and taps her fingers down the menu. "Yes, we'll have the eggs Benny, the blueberry waffles, the bagel and lox, home fries, and two sides of bacon."

The waitress regards me. "That's plenty, thank you."

She begins to walk away and Natalie calls her back. "Add chocolate chip pancakes to that order too." The waitress writes it on her pad and walks away.

"Hungry, Nat?" I ask, giving her an inquisitive look.

"I'm pregnant!" she blurts out.

I'm mid-swig and almost choke on the bubbles. "What? How? I mean, I know how. When? Wait. You were drinking," I scold.

"Oh, relax, you narc. I was pretending to drink it." She rolls her eyes at me.

"Natalie, this is amazing news—right?"

"Yeah, great news. I desperately want my perineum split from top to bottom."

She gives me a half-cocked grin.

"Can I stand up and announce it to the restaurant?" I ask jokingly.

"Sure, if you want to be drop-kicked in front of everyone you can."

"So that's a no then. Natalie, I'm so happy for you and Ben." It dawns on me that maybe he doesn't know. It wouldn't be out of character for Nat to dump him out of fear and do it on her own. "He knows, right?"

"Yes, of course he knows," she scoffs.

I hold my hands up in defense. "Okay, okay, I just had to ask." I clap my hands together with delight. "How far along are you?"

She looks down at her fingers and starts counting backwards under her breath. "About six weeks."

"That means . . ."

"Yup, that means first time back on the rod, and I get knocked up."

"Didn't you use a condom?" I give her a look of disapproval like a teacher in an after-school special.

"Nooo," she replies with attitude. "One minute he was doing the cookie dive, and doing a damn good job I might add, then—whammo—next thing I knew, I was begging him to get up in there. It had been so long, and it felt so good, I couldn't stop myself," she whines.

I cover my eyes with one hand and shake my head. Even after twenty years of friendship, she can still shock me with her candor.

"What did Benjamin say when you told him?"

She shrugs off my question. "He asked me to marry him," she answers matter of fact, almost appalled.

"What?" With wide eyes, I wiggle with excitement to the end of my chair. "Well, what did you say?"

"What did I say? I said, 'Are you fucking crazy?'" The couple sitting next to us looks over at her outburst.

"Natalie," I scorn her and apologize to the tables next to us. "Poor Benjamin, he must have been devastated."

She looks at me in shock "Poor Benjamin? What about poor Natalie? He's not the one with sore tits and puking his guts out every morning. I don't know how you did this, Jones."

I give her an understanding smile. Any uncertainty that I had about Natalie and I being normal again is gone. She is back at full speed. I reach across the table and give her hand a squeeze.

"I am so happy for you. You're going to be a great mother, Nat."

She pulls away from our embrace. Her brows are furrowed, and there's worry on her face.

"How do you know? I'm not like you, Jones. I'm selfish and impatient. I can barely take care of myself. How can I be responsible for another life?"

I take her hands in mine and laugh lightly.

"Natalie, did you listen to anything I said on the other side of that door? You're the most loving, kind, hard-ass woman I know. Look how amazing you are with Hope and Faith. They love you so much. And what you've done for my family over this last year? Words can't even begin to explain the indebtedness I have for you."

A little tear rolls down her face. "I'm so scared, Jones."

I squeeze both her hands for comfort. "You're supposed to be scared, sweetie. But trust me, the first time you hold that tiny person in your arms, you'll feel invincible. That's the moment you realize that you'll never put yourself first again." I stop and frown. "Well, maybe I'm not the best person to give you this advice."

"Jones, don't do that."

We're both teary-eyed now and hugging at the table. The couple at the next table looks over at us again.

"Hey, mind your own business, you two. Eat your pancakes," she accosts them.

"I don't know if I can do this." Her tearstained sable eyes meet mine.

"You can do this," I assure her. "You have me and Henry and Ben in your corner."

She bows her head and slumps her shoulders. "I don't know if I can do this."

After a moment, she visibly relaxes, sits up straight, and wipes her eyes with the cuff of her sleeve. "One thing I am sure of is this crying crap has got to stop. It's been going on for two weeks now."

Natalie hates not being in control. I know this vulnerability is really trying for her.

"Well, unfortunately the 'crying at the drop of a hat' phase will last pretty much through your entire pregnancy, but you'll be rewarded with the 'I can't get enough sex' hormones too. You will want Benjamin morning, noon, and night. You'll be mid-cereal-bite, and you'll need it right there on the counter."

She looks at me, amused. "Go on. Tell me more." She picks up her glass to take a drink.

I shoot her a castigating look.

"Dammit," Natalie replies. "Fine. Just take it away from me then."

We start laughing. The waitress is at our table with all the food—so much food. She places it all down, and I ask her to take away the bottle and the glasses. I won't drink, out of solidarity for Natalie. Plus, I have to drive home, so it's the best decision right now.

"So, what plans do you and Benjamin have now?"

"I'm not going to lie; I did feel bad when he left my place the night I told him off. We didn't speak at all the next day. I felt lost—lonely without him. I didn't have you to talk to." She gives me a snarl.

I respond with a pout.

"So two days go by, and I'm losing it by now. You know I don't handle rejection well, Jones."

"Really? I hadn't noticed."

"Ha-ha . . . you're so funny." She rolls her eyes at me. "Can I finish?"

I nod.

"I was about to pick up the phone to call him and give him a piece of my mind when the intercom buzzes. It was Benjamin. He was downstairs."

"Did you let him in?"

"Well, yeah, Jones, I'm not a total heartless bitch."

She's so exhausting.

"When I let him in, I was about to blast him for disappearing, but he beat me to it and says, 'Do you ever shut up?' Then he took me in his arms and dipped me low and kissed me."

"Can I tell you how much I love Benjamin right now, Nat?" I laugh.

"I figured you'd like that part." She huffs.

"Then what happened?"

"Then we sat and talked for hours about what the best setup would be for both of us during the pregnancy and after the baby is born."

"That's very mature of you. I'm so proud of you. What was the verdict?"

"He's moving into the loft—*but*, he's keeping his condo.

He is quite aware of my irreverence to conformity and the nuclear family. No offense, Jones."

"None taken and well done, Natalie. It's important to be open and honest right from the start. Did the conversation end well?"

She reaches into her pocket and extends a closed fist to me.

"Open your hand," she orders.

I'm confused, but I do as I'm told, and she places something in my palm. I look down to find a ring. Not just any ring. It's a brilliant black diamond, has to be at least three carat, attached to a metallic red band encrusted with black stones.

"Is this what I think it is?" I gush.

"I told him I would accept it as a commitment to parenthood together, not to marriage."

"You are one tough cookie, aren't you?"

She blows me a kiss. "Nice ring, though, don't you think?" She puts it on her ring finger and extends her hand out front to admire it.

"Uh, yeah—he must have spent a fortune on it. Not bad for a teacher's salary." I grab her hand and hold the diamond up to my eye to examine it closer.

"So, about that, it would seem that our Benjamin has some money."

I look at her dazed. "What kind of money?"

"Like money—like Onassis money. His grandfather was some big-time land owner in New Orleans and left him his fortune when he died."

"Well, well, well, look at little Natalie. Never in a million years would I have thought you would end up with a romantic Mr. Moneybags," I tease.

"I already told him I'm no kept woman. I make my own living. He can keep his money tucked away in his back pocket. I don't need any of it. Now, if he were to gift me, say, a pair of shoes or two along the way, I don't think I would decline."

She tries to keep a straight face while shoveling blueberry pancake in her mouth.

Looking at her, with a mouthful of food, I'm overcome with pure happiness that Natalie and I are back. The atrocious laceration that I caused in our relationship has been mended.

"Our babies are going to grow up together like we did, Nat. They will share the same bond we do."

"I know, and I wouldn't have it any other way, Jones."

15

Mom will be thrilled to hear about Natalie. I'm eager to get home to the girls and spend some much-needed playtime with them. They're not capable of judgment or scrutiny, but I still feel like I should apologize to them, as well. They've only ever shown love for me, even when I was at my worst. I suspect if I shower them with kisses and tickles, that will suffice for an apology. It will be interesting to see how they react to Mommy's new look though. From the day we brought them home, I've pretty much been living in comfy cotton with my dull, dirty blond hair pulled back in a messy bun.

I detour slightly and take the scenic route to enjoy the last few fall leaves before winter hibernation begins. Although I'm eager to get home to the girls and talk through some things with Mom before Henry gets back, I stop at the lighthouse for a few minutes of self-reflection. The sun is hovering over the horizon. A beautiful spectrum of oranges and blues and pinks shimmer on the calm waves of the lake water, reflecting up onto the thin clouds that halo the setting sun. I wrap my scarf tighter around my shoulders as shelter from the cold wind blowing off the water. I inhale the fresh, cold air deep into my lungs until I feel it fill every cell of my body.

I'm aware there is still a long road ahead of me. The snap of Rachel Kimble's fingers didn't make everything disappear, but it was just the push I needed to unshackle my chains that were holding me under my flood of deep despair. I respect Dr. Kennedy so much. He's my mentor, and he has been such a great support, helping me realize that I have the coping tools to get through this. But if it wasn't for Rachel, I don't know if Henry would have ever come into my life. All those years ago, she cleared the path for our meeting. Seeing her again was a thankful reminder.

I took for granted my ability to help others who suffer from many forms of mental conditions and social anxieties and other negative behavior patterns. I thought I could do it all on my own, and I ignored all of the signs and symptoms that I discuss with my patients regularly. In the process, I almost destroyed relationships with everyone I love. Although having studied psychology for years, now that I've experienced pain so personally, I'll be a much more valuable resource for my patients and display more empathy and understanding toward them. Oh, poor Mr. Smith, I'll need to personally apologize to him. My attitude with him was inexcusable. His last few sessions were probably not helpful at all, as I was filled with judgment.

This is part of the healing, understanding the impact my actions projected onto others, especially Henry. Our healing can't be clinical. It's deeper than that. We'll require an emotional cleanse.

Our souls are bonded forever, and what we went through is just another chapter in our story.

□ □ □

I'm home in time to bathe the girls, and good timing indeed. The girls, and the kitchen floor, are covered with green something or other. Mom is on her hands and knees wiping up the puree from the floor. The babies are, of course, giggling nonsensically because throwing food has become their new favorite game to play.

"Oh good. You're home. Can you grab me a wet cloth from the sink please, Izabel," she asks without looking up.

The girls are wiggling in their seats now with their little arms held high, requesting to be lifted out. I hand Mom the cloth. She sits back on her heels and brushes her hair out of her face with the back of her hand. Mom finally looks up at me and gasps.

"Izabel, you look gorgeous, honey." She rises and hugs me, but avoids touching me with her dirty hands.

"Let me have a look at you." She takes a step back and examines me.

"You like?" I ask, pumping my curls with both hands.

She nods. "Absolutely. But the question is: Do you like it?"

"I've never felt better, Mom. This was an important part of my transformation."

"Honey, if you're happy, I'm happy. That's all I've ever wanted for you. I knew you would find your way back when it was time. With tragedy comes clarity, but you can't put a time limit on that. As moms, we think we have to do it all, and if we fall, that somehow we've failed, but you have to fall in order to learn, my love, and this won't be the last time you fall. So many times when you were growing up, I second-guessed if I made the right decisions for you."

"You did great, Mom. I keep learning from you. Do you know how many times a day I stop and ask myself: 'What would Mom do right now?'"

Mom blushes. "Oh stop," she says as she pulls me into a hug. "We never stop learning, and we never stop second-guessing."

I relax in her arms and let her words of wisdom comfort me once again.

"Now take your babies up for a bath so I can clean this kitchen before your husband comes home," she orders.

I'm not even bothered that the girls have handled my hair and I'm covered in slop. I just want to squeeze them, I love them so much. Up in the en suite, I strip them down and toss their soiled clothes in the laundry basket and sit them in the oversized tub. The splashing starts as soon as the water hits their feet. I lean over the edge of the tub and watch them play. They both possess so many of Henry's features it's hard not to be mesmerized by them—their crystal green eyes and dark, curly hair, and then, of course, Faith's dimple. I place my finger on her chin and wiggle it. Her giggle makes my heart skip a beat.

"I miss your daddy, girls," I lament.

In between splashes, in unison, they both say, "Dada." They continue to say it and laugh.

138 | JB Lexington

This is incredible. Up until now, their conversations have consisted of babbling and pointing at objects they want, but now they're actually making connections. Henry usually gets in the bathtub with them. Now they are looking and calling for him. He'll be so excited, maybe a little sad that he missed it. But I guarantee he'll celebrate the fact they said "dada" before "mama." I guess I'll give him that.

Washed of the night's activities, I scoop the girls out of the tub and wrap them both in their hooded towels. Hope, of course, escapes and crawls down the hall, her little bottom wiggling back and forth. Faith lifts her arms so I'll pick her up. Hope knows her routine, all right; she's in the room, pulling the diapers and pj's out from underneath the changing table. She hasn't quite figured out how to dress herself, but that's not for a lack of trying. She's pulling at the diaper and trying to wrap it around her leg. Faith has no problem just lying back while we tend to her. She's never in a rush to do anything.

The girls fall asleep in my arms as we rock back and forth in the chair. I usually will put them down in their cribs after story time before they fall asleep. Henry is the pushover and holds them until they fall asleep. Tonight was different though. I didn't want to let them go. I needed their warmth and to feel the weight of them sink into me as they fell into their peaceful slumber.

□ □ □

"Hey, sleeping beauty."

I hear his voice and feel his warm breath on my face where the edge of my lips meets my cheek.

I open my eyes and try to focus, but the room is dark. "Am I dreaming?" I ask.

"You're not dreaming, Izzy. I'm home."

I arch my back a little to stretch. The girls are still curled up in my arms. I fell asleep in the chair with them.

"What time is it?" I ask Henry.

"It's just after two in the morning. I took the last flight home instead of waiting until the morning," he explains while picking up one girl at a time and putting them in their beds.

I watch him move around the dark room. He extends his hands to me and lifts me from the chair. He studies me.

"What do we have here?" he asks while rolling a crusty curl through his fingers.

"Makeover?" I answer more like a question. "Do you like it?"

"Very much." He smiles and plants a tender kiss on my lips.

Hand in hand, we walk down the hall to our bedroom.

"Henry, I just want to say . . ." I try to start my apology.

"Not tonight." He kisses me again. "I need you tonight, Izabel. We can do all the talking you want tomorrow, but tonight what I need is to feel you, to feel your touch, your kiss, your skin."

He tugs on my bottom lip ever so gently with his teeth. I respond with a moan. He pulls me in close until our bodies are flush. Our lips are locked, our tongues curling together, coaxing me deeper into his mouth.

We tear at each other's clothes. The carnal passion dominates our desire, ignoring all self-control. Henry lays me on the bed and unleashes a deep river of wet kisses up and down my neck.

"I love you so much, Izabel." His devoted decree almost sets me off.

I roll out from underneath the weight of him and straddle his midsection. Henry's hard cock is ready for me to mount. I slide down onto him slowly, savoring every inch of his manhood. He pulls me close and tugs a fistful of hair, moving me back and forth, up and down. He's the puppet master, and I'll do whatever he wants right now. I tilt forward onto his pelvis for added friction on my swollen clit. Coiling and rubbing, my climax is close.

His cock expands with every move, filling me completely, hitting my sweet spot every time I bang down on him. The pierce of his fingernails on the flesh of my bottom sends tremors between my legs. With unbridled hunger for him, I ride him wildly. "Henry, I'm coming!" I wail.

He continues to buck into me, holding me firm until I shatter on top of him, grunting until he finds his own end.

I collapse onto his chest, breathing heavily from my cathartic release.

"Welcome back," I coo after a couple deep breaths.

He gives me a playful smack on my bum. "I missed you."

I lift my lips to his and respond with a gentle kiss. "I'm back, Henry."

16

The sounds of laughter breach my morning REM sleep. Henry has the girls in bed, and he's playing patty-cake with them. I roll to face them.

"Mmm . . . this is my second favorite way to wake up," I say to him with my eyes still closed.

"Good morning to you too," Henry replies. "How was your sleep?"

"So restful." I stretch my arms above my head and respond through an aggressive yawn.

Henry laughs.

I shimmy up to a sitting position. "I have a present for you."

Henry's attention is piqued. "You do? What is it?"

"Hand me the girls, and I'll show you." I open my arms for the girls to come to my side of the bed. I sit them in my lap and kiss their little faces.

"Okay, girls, let's show Daddy what we learned yesterday." I point to Henry. "Who's that?" I ask excitedly. "Who's that?" I repeat again with a high-pitched tone. The girls start to squirm and begin their *dada-da-da-dada* mantra.

Henry's face lights up. "What does that mean?"

"Yeah, I figured you'd like that one. Go ahead and have your moment of glory." I roll my eyes at him and release the girls as Henry summons them back.

"Come to Dada, girls." He first showers Faith, then Hope, with kisses. "Who wants breakfast? *Dada* will make you breakfast." He looks at me with a gloat-filled smile.

His chin dimple is so pronounced right now under his morning scruff. He tucks both girls under each arm like footballs and zigzags out of the room.

"I'll get ready, and we'll drive in together," I shout out after him.

This will give us an opportunity to talk about what happened over the last few days. I can't assume that we're okay just because of what happened last night.

If I've learned anything from being a new mom, it's how to get ready in record time. With a final once-over in the mirror, I'm ready to go. I spray a few spritzes of dry shampoo and put fresh curls in my hair, apply a little blush and mascara, and I'm wearing one of my power suits—navy blue pinstripe pencil skirt and vest.

Down in the kitchen, Henry and Mom are singing breakfast songs to the girls. Mom sucked Henry into those early on. It's pretty cute to watch them dance around to his baritone sound.

Mom sees me first and gives me the thumbs up. "Good morning, Izabel."

"Hi, Mom."

Henry sends a wink my way. "You look great, Dr. Jones. I guess I'd better go put some effort into this." He waves his hand down his pajama-clad body. He kisses the tops of the girls' heads. "Say bye to Dada," he instructs them.

They erupt with multiple dadas like programmed little robots.

"You've created monsters. You know that, right?" I say to him.

"Yup," he replies happily.

□ □ □

The first twenty minutes of our drive are spent in a comfortable silence, but silence nonetheless. I suspect he's waiting for me to bring up the elephant in the room, as I should be the one.

I'm about to tell him that I went to see Rachel and how I realized that Tippy wasn't the trigger all along, and that I'll be scheduling regular appointments with Dr. Kennedy when I get into the office, but "Natalie's pregnant" blurts out of my mouth instead.

"I know," he says without taking his eyes off the road.

"Wait. What? How do you know?" I stutter confusedly.

"You were being a bit of an asshole, and she was dying to tell you, so she called me instead. She said I was the next best thing."

His sly grin is a display of both punishment and taunting with a dash of *na-na na-na boo-boo*.

I huff and pout in my seat. Henry reaches across and squeezes my hand.

"Henry, I'm sorry. I spent so much time consumed by my loss and how it impacted me that I didn't stop to think about anyone else. That wasn't fair to you. You had to take on the entire burden, and I didn't acknowledge your trauma." I bring his hand up to my face and rest it on my lips.

"I'm sorry. I'm sorry. I'm sorry." I kiss all over his hand through my wholehearted apologies.

"Okay, here's the deal, Izabel: From this point forward, there are no more apologies. I'll never ask you to forget what we went through that night because that is an extension of our forever together now. I chose you, and I'll choose you over and over again—every part of you, not just the good parts. We're going to heal together now. We'll see Dr. Kennedy together for as long as we need. We're not going to run away from our shadows anymore; they might have the answers we need."

I watch a teardrop that was brimming in his eye roll down the contour of his face and rest in the crease of his nose. I lean across into his space and kiss the moisture off his face. The taste of his salty tear is like an elixir that has been injected directly into my heart.

Henry clears his throat, followed by a couple of sniffles. "Okay, so we're in this together. Deal?" He lifts his hand for me to give him a high-five.

I smack his hand and giggle. "Deal." It feels good to laugh with him after the events of the last week.

"Do you have a busy day?" Henry inquires.

"I do, actually. As you know, I've been a little absent lately, so anyone that I had rescheduled are all coming in today. You don't mind picking me up a little later, do you?" My admission of dereliction of duty was disappointing, yet refreshing.

"Of course not, babe. I can always find work to do at the office."

"There is one more thing." The confident tone in my voice is certain.

"What's that?" he asks as he turns the final corner before my office building.

"I'm meeting Tippy for lunch today."

Henry pulls into the drop-off area in front of the office building and puts the car in park.

The look of worry on his face when he regards me is warranted. I find comfort in knowing that he'll always be concerned. It makes me feel safe and protected.

"Do you think it's a good idea to see her before the trial?"

"Yeah, I do. This is it, the final piece to the puzzle. I've been lost in the sounds of the silence between us since the tragedy of Bo's death, and I can't let it keep me hostage anymore. She must be in so much pain, and I want to give her the opportunity to free herself of the guilt that she harbors—the guilt of what happened to you, to our family."

"I trust your judgment, Dr. Jones." He leans over and kisses me tenderly. "If you need more time, just send me a quick text. I'll come whenever you're ready."

"Thanks, my love. Have a great day." With one leg out the door, I turn back to him before I leave to start my day. "And Henry—thank you."

He winks at me as I shut the door, and then he drives off.

□ □ □

Walking through the staff hall on the fifteenth floor, Dr. Kennedy and I acknowledge each other.

"Are we on for tomorrow, Dr. Jones?" he inquires.

"You got it, Dr. K.," I respond with my most chipper tone. I'll have to explain the last few weeks to him and that I went to see Rachel but that it actually helped push me through the fog. He'll be pleased with any form of therapy that was successful.

The first sight I always have when I open my office door is of Dottie's big, pink lipstick-stained smile. She's such a wonderful lady. I couldn't ask for a better person to help keep me organized and scheduled. What she's done for me is invaluable. The excuses she's had to concoct, the last-minute cancellations, and having to field flustered patients. I should never have put her in such a position.

"Good morning, Dr. Jones," she chirps.

"Hi, Dottie. How was your weekend?"

"It was lovely. Thanks for asking. Let me grab you a cuppa tea." She begins to roll her chair away from her desk.

"No, please sit. I'll make one for the two of us," I offer sweetly.

She nods in agreement and slides her chair back, but taps her watch, warning me of my time. We keep a small kettle and some mugs in our office so we don't have to go to the communal kitchen when the craving strikes. I unwrap the English Breakfast tea bags, drop them in, and tie the string around the porcelain handle. I hear soft music coming from her phone, a low drawl of the harmonies of two male singers accompanied by the sounds of a guitar and fiddle. It's quite soothing.

"What's that you're listening to?"

"Oh it's nothing, just an old Scottish love song. Let me turn it off." Dottie handles her phone to stop the music from playing.

"It sounds beautiful. Can you leave it on for me to hear until the tea is ready?"

A smile touches the corners of her mouth and plays in the laugh lines beside her eyes. "Of course, Dr. Jones."

"What do the lyrics mean?" The melody is so delicate that the lyrics must clutch the heart.

Dottie thinks about it for a minute and turns up the volume slightly. "Love was driven by distance back then," she begins to explain. "Lovers were separated by wars and land discovery. He's professing his love for her—that he will tame the most vicious seas and trudge barren lands to be back by her side. That he longs to hear the laughter from under her feet as she dances like a fairy around the fires that light the night skies."

Her reverie is halted by the sound of the hissing kettle, and she seems embarrassed by it.

It dawns on me there might be two hearts clutched in this room.

"Wow!" I exclaim and hand her the cup of tea.

"It's lovely, isn't it, deary? This old gal can pick a tune." She winks. "Now go on. You have a busy day ahead of ya."

17

Bo and I have been divorced for over six years and I'm still worried about being late to meet Tippy. I look down at my watch. It's 1:20 p.m. Only five minutes late. I smile as I pass the valet and rush through the front door of Chez Nous. I'm greeted by Miguel, the maître d'. He has worked here for as long as I can remember. I've learned so much about him and his family over the years. He has three children, two daughters and a son. His wife, Lola, works as a nurse in a senior assisted living center, and his dog, Rocky the Boxer, only has three legs. I'm sure he doesn't recognize me now though. I haven't been here for over a year, not since Bo's sister's bridal shower lunch.

"Welcome to Chez Nous. Do you have a reservation?" he asks.

"Hi, Miguel. It's Izabel." I smile sweetly at him.

He tilts his head to one side and analyzes my face. "Ah . . . Izabel. Hola, hermosa dama. Como esta?" How are you, pretty lady? He gives me a double-cheek kiss. "It's been so long." He takes my hands in his and lowers his eyes. "I'm so sorry to hear about Mr. Bo. He was a good man, he was." His expression is somber.

"Thank you, Miguel. That's very kind of you to say."

"Mrs. Carmichael is here already."

"Of course she is already here," I mumble under my breath.

"Let me show you to your table, please." He gestures for me to follow him.

I follow him through the sea of tables to Tippy's usual spot. It's always a table for four in the center of the restaurant. Her fishbowl, we used to call it. She gets the most exposure there. There she can conduct simultaneous conversations. As petite as she is, I spot her immediately. She stands when we reach the table. Her hair is spectacularly coiffed, and her charcoal Donna Karen pant suit is a perfectly tailored fit for her frame.

"Izabel, darling," she says. Instead of her double-cheek air kiss, she hugs me close, catching me off guard. We stand in what should feel like an awkward embrace, but it's rather comforting. Even when she was my mother-in-law, we were never this genuine. Miguel stands to the side and patiently waits for us so he can usher us into our seats.

She holds me at arm's length to assess my . . . hair, outfit, and shoes, probably all of it.

"You look fabulous, Izabel. Your face is glowing." Even her compliments are heartfelt.

Miguel seats us, and then returns to the reception area.

Without asking if I would like a drink, she motions for our waiter to pour me a glass from her Bloody Mary pitcher. I was going to stick with coffee, but the least I can do is have a drink with her.

"Are you hungry, Izabel darling?" She looks down at the one-page menu.

"Starved actually." I rub my belly as it grumbles. It's been weeks since I remember actually enjoying a meal.

"We'll have our usual, Stefan," she orders the waiter without acknowledging him. He's been hovering around the table in anticipation of the snap of her fingers.

"Of course, Ms. Carmichael." He bows and retreats to the kitchen. The Cobb salad wasn't going to be my first choice, but Tippy choosing what I eat for lunch today is trivial in the grand scheme of the purpose of our meeting.

We sit in an uncomfortable silence for a few minutes. She fidgets and adjusts the midsection of her jacket and then smooths out the side of her perfectly set hair. She assesses the room to see who from her social circle is also dining here today, and if I know Tippy, she's scanning to see who might be looking at her.

"So, Izabel, how are your children?" she inquires flatly. I know she knows their names, but her indifference doesn't bother me.

"They're great—growing like little weeds. They're ten months old now. Hope, she's a few minutes older, is desperate to walk. She pulls herself up to a standing position every chance she gets and takes a step or two before she ends up on the ground again. Faith is a different story. She's the younger one. That little peanut, she'd be content being carried around like a fluffy purse dog. And they have such unique personalities already. They said 'dada' the other day. Henry would not stop gloating about it."

Suddenly I'm aware I've lingered lovingly for too long. I pick up my glass and take a drink in efforts to give Tippy an opportunity to take control of the conversation.

Instead, back-and-forth smiles are exchanged.

"How is Jack doing?"

"Jack is very busy. He's been leading a gun-reform committee since . . ." She pauses to take a drink. "But he has to tread lightly, or the GOP might think he's crossing over to the radical left."

I sense sarcasm in her update.

"Although, I don't think anyone could accuse him of moving left. Let's just say Jack wishes the shooting would have happened out of state, a little farther south." The sinister tone in her declaration would be believable if it wasn't for the agony in her eyes. She tips her head back and drains the last drop of reddish-orange liquid from her glass. Then she holds up her crystal goblet and rattles the remaining ice cubes. Her attentive servant is instantly by her side, topping up her chosen panacea.

I regard her with a regretful look for asking the question.

"Tippy, are you okay?" I ask cautiously.

"Of course I'm not okay, Izabel." She huffs at me.

Before she can continue, Stefan appears at the table with our salads.

"Salt or pepper for either of you ladies?" he asks.

"No, that will be all," she says and dismisses him with a wave of her hand.

She picks up her fork and knife and begins to cut the lettuce in the bowl in front of her.

Without looking at me, she continues, "My son is dead. How should I feel, Doctor?"

I'm taken aback by her bitter comeback.

"I'm so sorry, Tippy. I didn't mean to upset you."

"Darling, you didn't upset me. My son being shot in cold blood is what's upset me. My husband paying more attention to his son now that he's dead is what's upset me. Jack using Bo to push his goddamn political agenda is what's upset me." She throws her cutlery down on the table and pushes her bowl away. Her hands shake, and she brings the goblet up to her mouth. She drinks until her glass is empty again.

My heart aches for this frail, broken woman. The desperation in her voice is soul crushing. I'm so angry at Jack. That man has always made my blood boil over. I can't hold back the tears that have welled up in my eyes.

Tippy regards me with a compassionate expression. She's composed again, looking around as if to collect her thoughts. "Now, now, Izabel. The time for crying is over. Tears won't bring Bo back. I'm sure you can agree that he will be forever in our memories, the good ones and the bad."

All the years living a life with a hard exterior shell have stripped her of the ability to mourn her child properly. I want to hug her and tell her to let it go, to release the demons that are devouring her, mentally and physically.

I reach across the table and give her fragile, perfectly manicured hand a comforting squeeze. Her gaze was stormy, but there was more there, a profound sadness and vulnerability that made her seem less rigid.

She pulls her bowl back and takes a minuscule bite of lettuce and then places her fork back down. I take her lead as permission to eat, as well.

"Izabel, please tell me about Henry. The poor dear, how is he healing?" she asks as I'm mid-bite.

I chew a few times before I attempt to respond. "He's doing better." I keep my answer short, trying not to come across as insensitive.

"Elaborate, Izabel. Honestly, I'd like to hear about his progress. I was very worried for you and your family."

I prestructure my narration to recount the last ten months to avoid miring in unnecessary minutia. Keeping it clinical is best, I think.

We eat and chat for the remainder of our lunch meeting, and I was happy to see Tippy actually finish the contents of her bowl. I, on the other hand, would have licked the bowl clean if I wasn't in public.

I know the intention for our lunch today was for Tippy to ask me again if I would attend the murder trial. She didn't bring it up the entire lunch, but I feel obligated to give her an explanation as to why I can't go. I don't think it will come as much of a surprise to her, but she deserves an explanation nevertheless.

Before I can get the words out, she interjects. And as if I'm holding a crystal ball, she says, "I'll completely understand if you don't come to the trial. You and your family have been through enough, unfortunately because of Bo. I don't expect you to continue to relive the horror. Jack Carmichael is on the case, and he'll make sure the most severe sentencing will be handed out, and I just have to find comfort in that." Her pause is thought-filled.

"Izabel, I quite enjoyed having you as a daughter, and I want to apologize if I ever made you feel insignificant. Bo treated you very poorly. I knew it, and I should have done something about that. I made peace with my decisions early on in my marriage, and I think I found comfort knowing that you shared my silent affliction. I'm very happy for you. Henry is a wonderful man, and your baby girls personify hope and faith to their fullest. I would really like to continue to be part of your lives, if you'll have me."

Her sincere appeal has made my eyes well up again. This time she reciprocates and allows a tear to break loose.

And just like that, at the bottom of a forty-dollar Cobb salad, Tippy found resolution.

18

My faithful milk alarm clocks never fail. I look at the bedside clock. It's 6:00 a.m., right on time. I begin to rustle out of bed. Henry murmurs, "I'll go."

"It's okay. You sleep, honey. I have to breastfeed anyway. I'm full this morning, and sore."

He rolls back over, pulls the duvet over his shoulders, and resumes his slumber.

The girls are at full attention when I get to them. If my boobs hadn't woken me, they weren't far behind.

"Good morning, my sweet girlies," I sing.

They wave their little hands at me in anticipation of the treat to come. Hope has somehow managed to wiggle one arm out of her jumper. Her little cherub-like skin is too tempting. I have to shower it with kisses. Faith has sat back down as she waits her turn. I take it for granted that she hasn't a care in the world being second, always. *Take a mental note, Izzy. Remember to make Hope wait her turn. She needs to learn some patience.*

I wonder where she gets that characteristic from?

Adorned with fresh nappies and pj's, we're finally ready for a liquid breakfast. We're on the precipice of breastfeeding ending. They're growing out of their baby yoga poses I twist them into to feed them at the same time, and now they just use my boobs for fun, not nutrition. They carry on while they suckle like little hummingbirds at a feeder, but as much as I love this morning routine with them, it's time to retire "the girls."

"We'll just have to find a new morning routine. Isn't that right, girls? Maybe one that involves Daddy getting up at six every morning." They simultaneously drop my nipple and release a milk-drunk slur, and call *dada*.

□ □ □

I sneak back into the bedroom, so as to not wake Henry, and head straight for our en suite. He's already in the shower. I strip down and take a silent moment to admire his naked form. The muscles on his back and shoulders rippling as he washes his hair, the sudsy water running down his face, dripping from his perfect mouth and pooling into his sexy dimple. I don't remember a time now without the knotted scars on his body. They have become part of who he is—part of us. My eyes glaze over as I savor every minute of this Adonis that is my husband.

As quietly as possible, I open the glass door and slide in behind him. I wrap my arms around his waist and rest my cheek on his back. His body is soothingly warm. He flinches from the unexpected adoration, but then he stretches his arms behind me and pulls me closer so our bodies are flush together.

Completely content, we stand motionless, the water cascading down around us, washing away the affliction that has ruled us both in our own extraordinary way.

Without breaking our embrace, Henry turns to face me and rests his forehead on mine. His gaze is fixed deep into me, restoring and healing the true essence of my being. I bite my lip momentarily to subdue my instant carnal hunger and then tilt my head back, inviting his lips down to mine. His tender kisses are unmasked only by passionate longing. My tongue plunges to the back of his mouth, wanting more of him—all of him. I drag my fingernails down the contour of his spine, and then with one hand resting on his lower back, I move the other hand between us and gently squeeze his full arousal, praising it with long, generous strokes. He releases a slow, gracious moan into my mouth and tightens his grip around my body.

"I've missed this," Henry whispers, a low vow on my lips.

Lifting both my legs effortlessly around his waist, he takes a couple of steps until I'm secure against the mosaic-tiled wall of the shower. I guide him into me, and slowly he fills me, inch by inch by inch, our eyes locked. Resting his full body weight between my legs, he stills; our bodies, our souls, become one. We match breath for breath. Any trace of anguish is replaced by euphoria, and for the second time in my life, I fall completely and madly in love with Henry. This is where we belong forever, entwined and making delicious, unhurried love to one another.

Wrapped in our towels, we scurry back to the bed so we can steal a few more minutes of alone time together.

The winter sun barely peeks out from behind the clouds, but a stray ray beams through the window, casting a soft amber glow around the room.

"Don't move," Henry instructs me. He props himself up on his elbow and stares at me lovingly.

"You look so beautiful in this light, Izabel. You always look beautiful. But right here, right now, in the pale haze of the dawn, you've never looked more perfect."

I close my eyes and absorb the warmth of the sunlight and the sentiment of Henry's adoration.

I feel his warm lips graze my eyelids. He continues kissing my face down to the small depression at the bottom of my neck. Then Henry opens my towel, exposing me. I hear the hiss of his inhale through his teeth. His strong hand kneads my supple breasts, and he inches down my body until he's between my legs. I spread my legs willingly, and his fingers find my wetness. He massages and pulls at my swollen lips before sliding a finger in, penetrating me over and over. He introduces his thumb and begins swirling around my sensitive tip. My body is quivering, already too close to climax. I moan and Henry eases off my clit. *Don't come yet*, I hear him say. Stealthily, he slithers down between my legs, and I'm rewarded with his hungry tongue lapping up my flowing excitement. I wrap my finger through his messy locks and anchor him in place; my hips move with the cadence of his feast. He pulls me in closer by my legs, not wanting to miss a drop of my pleasure. He's unrelenting and continues his onslaught of drinking me in until I come again and again. I try to contain my orgasm, but I release the most ferocious groan, followed by a few calming purrs.

He slides back up my body, gently resting his weight on me, and bestows upon me a tender kiss with his delicious, glistening lips.

Back in the en suite, I massage moisturizer into my face. Henry's standing next to me, brushing his teeth. "Hey, you do have your own side of the vanity, you know. Why are you standing right next to me?" I tease and attempt to push him out of my space. He winks and spits minty foam into my sink.

"Not to ruin the mood, but how did your meeting with Tippy go?" he inquires with caution.

"It went really well, actually. I think she was able to find some closure. At least I hope so. She wants to stay involved in our lives, and I told her okay. Are you okay with that?"

"Of course, Izzy. She's a lovely lady, and I want nothing but peace and happiness for her. If spending some time with you and the girls is what she needs, then we'll be there for her."

"You're so good, Henry."

"Oh, I know I'm good," he jokes.

□ □ □

I sit on the sofa with a ridiculous post-orgasmic grin splashed across my face. Hope is playing on the activity mat on the floor in front of me. I hear slapping hands on the hardwood coming down the hall. Faith pops her head around the corner. It's a funny thing—the girls are identical, but when I see Faith's wee face, it takes my breath away. I see Henry every time I look at her.

"Come here, baby girl. Come see Mama."

"Faith," I hear my mom holler.

"I have her, Mom. She's okay." Faith makes her slow crawl over to me and pulls herself up my legs. She squeals with pride when she finally stands straight. Her little sausage legs jiggle as she tries to steady.

"Yay—look at my big girl—good for you!" I clap my hands with delight for her. Faith giggles. The sheer innocence behind her beautiful green eyes mesmerizes me and puts me at complete ease. Her long lashes flutter like the wings of a butterfly's first flight out of its cocoon while she babbles her dialog of pride to me. I pick her up and hold her in my arms above my head and give her a congratulatory shake. Henry comes in and scoops her up and flies her around the room.

"You're coming with me, little one. Mama has to go to work now." His singsong tone mocks my departure.

I put on my shoes and grab my purse to leave. Henry has both girls scooped up under his arms. "Say bye to Mommy—we'll miss you." It's days like today when I never want to leave.

I'm about to walk out when Henry calls after me. "Izabel, you don't have patients tomorrow, right?"

"Right," I confirm, curious where this is going.

"Okay, don't make any plans. I have something fun for us to do."

My heart flutters like a seventh-grade schoolgirl getting passed a love note. I respond with a smile and head out to start my day.

19

The next morning, I'm up early, not only for my usual routine, but from the anticipation of not knowing what Henry has planned for us today. I can't even endeavor a guess. He hasn't hinted at all, nor have we discussed anything that would merit any kind of speculation.

I put the girls back in their cribs after their morning feeding so I can rush back to my room and get ready for the day. I step inside and see on my bed is a suitcase. I look around, but I don't see Henry. Then he comes out of the bathroom, his towel loosely wrapped around his waist, hanging just above his pubic line. I focus in on his hairline that trails down to his . . . *No, focus, Izabel.*

"Why is my suitcase out?" I ask suspiciously. "Are we going somewhere?"

He doesn't answer; he just continues to shake the excess water from his hair.

"How am I supposed to know what to pack? You can't spring a surprise like this on a girl—we have outfits and shoes and accessories that have to be carefully thought out for days, usually weeks—before a holiday." I rush into the walk-in and begin swiping through hangers. I grab my black ankle booties and my knee-high, camel-color boots. I have my Mary Jane peep toes hanging from my fingers.

Henry begins to laugh. I throw the shoes on my bed.

"Jones, I've already packed for you," he says, pointing to the suitcase.

"What do you mean you've packed for me? That's a carry-on. Nothing fits in a carry-on. Where're we going—a nudist colony?" I ask, throwing my hands up.

Henry drops his towel. "Yup, and I'm ready to go."

"Ha-ha. You knew when you married me that spontaneity stresses me out, Henry Rudolph. Now please tell me where we are going so I can pack properly."

He pulls his Calvin Kleins out of his dresser and puts them on. Then he stands in front of me now and takes my hands into his.

"Do you trust me?" he asks adorably.

I let out an appeasing sigh. "Yes."

"Everything you need is in here, okay? We're only gone for one night. A night you won't want to miss."

I reach down and hook my finger on the zipper and mimic opening it.

"Okay?" he asks again.

"Okay," I reply with a long drawl like a bratty kid being told to pick up her toys.

"Hurry up now or we'll miss our flight." Henry nonchalantly walks into his corner of the closet and puts on his jeans—*the ones that make his ass look incredible*—and a fitted black V-neck knit sweater. It seems we're going casual. That should make it easier for me to pick out my outfit. He walks out with his suit bag draped over his shoulder.

"What's with the suit?" I ask.

"We're going to want to celebrate later tonight. All you need to do is get dressed right now," he orders playfully.

"Well, what will I have on while you're wearing your suit later tonight at this mystery event we're going to?" This guessing game is getting old fast, and it's too early for me to be this miffed. He's enjoying every minute of it though. I can see it in his foxy grin.

"Everything you'll need is in your suitcase. When have I ever steered you wrong when it comes to your outfits?"

He's not wrong. He has a knack for picking out a woman's outfit. I think he enjoys shopping for my clothes more than I do.

"Fine," I concede.

"Now, was that so hard?" He gives me a playful smack on the ass. "Meet me downstairs in a half hour. I'll get the girls up. Your mom will be here in twenty minutes."

Moping, I walk into the bathroom. "Half hour, who only gets a half hour to get ready?"

"I love you!" Henry shouts back at me. I sense a mocking tone.

"Yeah, yeah, say that again when I know where we're going."

I let the warm water envelop my body as I grin from ear to ear.

□ □ □

We pull into the parking garage at Chicago O'Hare at ten.

Henry still hasn't broken his silence about our destination. At least one piece of the puzzle is solved. We're flying somewhere. Life with Henry has always been an adventure, I'll give him that. I roll my carry-on beside me through the maze of the airport until we get to the departures. Henry has already pre-checked us in to our flight. We sit in the waiting area, and I look around at the gate numbers and the cities listed on the boarding signs. Dallas. Pittsburgh. New York. Nashville. We could be going anywhere.

"Are you going to tell me yet?" My question is filled with a combination of exhilaration and frustration.

He turns a pretend lock and key on his lips and gestures throwing it away.

Henry hands me a gossip magazine, which I can only assume is a token of apology for the covert operation. I flip through the pages while we wait for our flight to be called.

I'm midway through an article about the Real Housewives from somewhere or other and their fight about who's lying about a facelift when I hear a boarding announcement.

"Good morning. We're going to begin boarding American Airlines flight 1625 to Dallas."

I wait for Henry's reaction; he looks at me and shakes his head no.

At least I'll find out if she got the facelift or not. I go back to reading. A few minutes later, the sound of the crackling speaker is in my ear again. With so many advancements in the world, why can't airports figure out a better sound system?

"Good morning, passengers of Delta Airlines. This is the first boarding call for flight number 424 to

New York, LaGuardia. Please have your boarding passes ready for the gate."

Henry places his hand on my leg and squeezes. "That's us."

I squeak with excitement and hop out of my seat. I toss the magazine into my tote and hurry Henry to line up with me.

Our bags are stowed, and we're nestled in our seats. I make all my necessary adjustments. I wait for Henry to do the same.

"Now will you tell me what's going on?" I'm almost begging now.

His giddiness is palpable. "I'll tell you a little bit. When we get there, we'll grab a yellow cab to the Plaza, check in, and then we're going to have brunch in the Champagne Bar and drink mimosas."

I clap with excitement.

"I knew you'd like that. Then the real fun begins at 4:00 p.m. sharp. That's all I'm going to tell you, so sit back, put in your ear buds, and forget about it."

□ □ □

My avocado toast was probably the best I've ever had. It was topped with crispy chickpeas and smooth ricotta. The two mimosas put me in the perfect relaxed state. I lie on the oversized king bed in our suite, rubbing my full belly. It feels so good to do nothing for just a minute. I close my eyes and inhale the scent of lavender that's coming from somewhere in the room.

Henry drops his face to mine and kisses my forehead. "Satisfied?"

"Mmm, I will be." I reach my hand in between his legs.

"You're cute." He places my hand back on my belly. "You should nap. You deserve it. Look at this huge bed you'll have all to yourself for an hour." His tempting offer is welcomed.

"What are you going to do?" I ask without opening my eyes.

"I'm going to get a workout in before we have to leave. I'll see you soon."

I mumble something incoherent and roll to my side. I grab the edge of the fluffy duvet and wrap it around me and gladly succumb to the pillow-top comfort.

The sound of ice cubes clinking in a glass wakes me out of my comatose state. I'm still wrapped in the duvet on the same spot on the bed. I can't remember the last time I napped worry-free. I feel very rested. I lean up on my elbow and watch Henry putter around the room.

"Are you drinking a whiskey in the middle of the afternoon?" I scold playfully.

"I'm celebrating," he says and raises his glass.

"And what is it exactly you're celebrating?" I flash him my best flirty smile in hopes to break him.

"Stay tuned." He winks. "You should stop asking questions and get ready. We have to leave in an hour."

Suddenly I'm panicked because I remember I don't know what's in the suitcase. What if I ate too much and it's too tight or he didn't bring the right bra or stockings? I jump out of bed, grab my bag, and disappear into the bathroom.

"One hour!" Henry shouts after me.

"You're infuriating, Henry Rudolph."

"But you love me."

That is a true statement.

Henry calls out from the other room. "How much more time do you need, Iz, so I know when to call the concierge to bring a car around for us?"

"Just a few more minutes." I give a final look-over to check my hair and makeup. How does he do it? Everything he packed, you would think he pulled straight off a mannequin that had my exact measurements. He dug deep in the back of my closet for this one. I love him for thinking it still fits me. Henry bought this black cocktail dress for me a couple of years ago for a fancy New Year's party we were invited to. I didn't get to wear it though because I got food poisoning from a bad turkey sandwich I ate at lunch that day. I was sick in bed all night. Henry stayed awake until midnight so he could kiss my forehead and wish me a Happy New Year. I spent the next two days in bed recovering. He was by my side the entire time, rubbing my back and bringing me warm water and crackers. I jolt out of my loving reverie—*what if it doesn't fit*. I quickly step into it and inch the fabric up my body. I check every angle I can in the mirror, looking for any lumps or rolls. Hmm. This dress does look great on me. I fill it out a bit more now, but the material is somewhat forgiving, so I'm not bothered. It's a fit black pencil dress with a straight neckline attached to slim straps, with a cute ruffle slit up the right leg. It shows just enough thigh. He packed me black lingerie and nude Cuban-heel stockings. A go-to favorite of Henry's for a night of pleasure. I have to admit I feel so sexy and regal when I wear them, like I should be lying on a chaise, wearing a silk robe, smoking a cigarette out of one of those gold filters, and drinking eight-hundred-dollar champagne.

I open the door and Henry is leaning against the wall waiting for me. He's decked out in his charcoal suit and slim black tie. That's my equivalent of the Cuban stockings.

I hear a little hitched gasp. "Izabel. You're gorgeous. You always take my breath away but this is—Wow." He holds his hand over his heart.

My cheeks flush instantly at his ardent admiration for me. "Well, you ain't too shabby either," I joke, or I fear I might cry at his overwhelming affection for me at this moment.

He pulls me in close and kisses me deep down to my soul. Our tongues dance around, seeking pleasure.

He holds me at arm's length now. "Phew. Okay, we gotta go, or I'm going to tear this dress off you and take you right up against the wall."

We lean on opposite walls as we gain our composure.

He hands me my coat. "Let's go, sexy."

The limo pulls around, and the driver gets out and makes his way to the passenger side of the car. He holds the back door open for Henry and me. We drive for twenty minutes or so, and then we stop in front of a building I don't recognize. The trees lining the street reflect off the glass-clad front. Then I see the big illuminated sign: Sotheby's. Henry and I walk through the revolving doors. A man dressed in a tuxedo hands him a catalog and a paddle. I shoot Henry an inquisitive look.

"Just go with it."

Once inside the connecting room, we find two empty seats on the left side near the front. The room is buzzing with people I can only imagine are the likes of art collectors, curators, and possibly celebrities. There are pieces of art hung on every spare space of the walls. Some artists I recognize; others I don't. Thumbing through the catalog, I see exorbitant prices flash by me. Twenty thousand, two hundred thousand—one million. The prices get higher the farther into the catalog I flip.

"Henry, what are we doing here?"

"Shhh," he responds. "They're about to start. Watch the podium." He hands me the paddle with the number eighty-four on it. A tall, blond, slim lady, in her early thirties, dressed impeccably in a tailored suit, stands before the crowd at the podium on the elevated platform at the front of the room. I look at Henry for guidance, and all he offers is a wink. The auction attendees are still and composed, except for the quiet buzz of preparedness, but the chaos of the situation is incomprehensible to me right now.

"Ladies and gentlemen, if you could all please turn to page eight in your catalog. First up for bid this evening is item number seventeen." Her British accent echoes through the silence. "A painting titled *After Eve*, by American artist Charles Rudolph. Please let the bidding begin at ten thousand. Do I hear ten thousand? Ten thousand. Thank you. How about fifteen thousand? Yes, thank you. Fifteen thousand. Now twenty thousand. Do I hear twenty thousand?"

Henry nudges my arm to lift my paddle. I'm so confused yet mesmerized by my uncertainty. I look at him and he nods. He whispers to me, "Go ahead. Bid on it. You'll want this."

I'm struck by excitement now. I raise my paddle. "Thank you. Twenty thousand to the lady to the left. Twenty-five thousand. We're at twenty-five thousand."

Someone from the back shouts twenty-two thousand, evoking a competitive nature I did not know I had. I didn't know this painting of Eve existed, and now I don't want anyone else to have it. I counter and raise my paddle and shout, "Twenty-six thousand!"

"Yes, thank you. Twenty-six thousand again to the lovely lady to the left. Do I hear thirty thousand?" There's a pause as she looks around the room. "Going once, going twice . . ." She scans the room for a final time. She slams her gavel on the podium. "Sold to the lovely lady on the left for twenty-six thousand dollars."

A handler wearing white gloves appears on stage beside the auctioneer and removes the painting from the easel and disappears behind the curtain.

She continues on, "Please now turn your catalog to page number eleven."

Henry taps me on the shoulder and whispers in my ear, "Let's go."

We sneak out to the foyer, hand in hand, and sit on the polished concrete bench outside the grand doors.

I wait a few seconds until I know the door has closed completely as to not disturb the auction. "Are you going to tell me what's going on now? Why did I just buy one of Charlie's paintings—for twenty-six thousand dollars, by the way?"

"The morning I left after our fight, I went straight to my parents' place. I started looking through Granddad's things again. For what, I don't know. Advice, guidance, a sign that you and I would be okay. I was flipping through his journal, and I came across Eve's name. It didn't faze me, obviously, because we know the story now, but it was dated Detroit 1930, the year after he and my grandmother were married. Here, I took a photo of the page so you could read it."

He holds his phone up for me to look at, and I snatch the phone from Henry's hands in disbelief and tap on the screen to make the image bigger. Then I begin to read the scratchy cursive.

I sketched Eve today. I watched her from afar while she stood outside of the Blue Note. The sky was filled with sunshine, but dark shadows circled her. She appeared lost and without life. How I wish I could go to her and tell her of my life now—After Eve. I wanted to run to her and tell her that not a day has passed that I don't long to wrap her in my embrace, to feel her sweet breath on mine, that she continues to tug at my heart. I'm a stump of a man to allow this beautiful human to be encumbered by such dismay. She holds the key to the secrets holding me. Eve will forever be in my dreams.

I'm completely dumbfounded. "How . . . ? What . . . ? How did you find the painting?"

"After I read this, I started doing searches for Charles Rudolph paintings. I was scrolling through, and then I found it. I clicked on the photo, and it took me to Sotheby's website, and there it was in the auction catalog. That was our sign, Izabel. Eve was his true love, and he lived without her and took that to his grave with him. I never want to be without you." Henry caresses my face and tucks a stray hair behind my ear.

"This belongs with us, Izzy, to remind us that it's you and me forever." He rests his forehead to mine, and we sit, enjoying the silence of the heaviness of this new discovery.

My heart aches for Eve once again. How different her life would have been, if only. Her entire life was sacrificed for us. If it weren't for Eve, I wouldn't have Henry; I wouldn't have my family.

"Do we get to take it with us now?"

Henry smiles. "No, we just have to wait for the clerk and confirm our information, and they'll ship it to us.

A wave of disappointment runs through me. Now that I own this piece of Charlie and Eve's history, I suddenly feel very overprotective of it. I want to shout into this open space and hear the echoes of my happiness reverberate off the concrete walls.

"What do we do now?" I ask innocently.

Henry leans in and lingers a long, loving kiss on my lips. "This is New York fucking City, baby—we can do whatever you want."

20

It's been a couple of weeks now since Henry and I went to New York. I caught myself smiling today for no reason, and then I realized it was because I was thinking about him. There was a rekindling that I can't explain. In a hundred lifetimes, or any version of reality, the energy that was flowing between us at the realization that Charlie and Eve are responsible for our entire existence was so powerful that we couldn't keep our hands off one another. We made love all night until the dawn broke. I've been dying to tell Nat about everything. Well, not everything—okay, probably everything—but about the painting especially and the story behind it, but I didn't want to do it over the phone.

We invited Natalie and Benjamin over for dinner tonight for the big reveal. Also it will be a pre-Christmas dinner because she won't be around this year; she's going to meet Ben's parents for the first time—swollen belly and all. She wants to pretend it's Christmas Eve with the girls tonight. She says she has another perfect gift for them. I can only imagine what it is this time.

At 5:00 p.m. on the dot, Natalie's at the door, with Benjamin standing behind her. She's doing her usual knock.

Well it's not so much a knock as a drumbeat she does on the door once she's already entered the house. We do have a bedroom made up especially for her at all times, so knocking to come in was never established.

"Hey, Nat, you're early, and by early I mean you're on time. That's unusual for you."

She huffs at me like I've released the most atrocious lie about her.

"So rude, Jones. Don't talk shit about me in front of my baby daddy." Natalie covers his ears in jest.

"Hi, Ben." I lean in and give him a welcoming hug. "So nice to see you again."

He hands me a gorgeous fall floral arrangement with vibrant yellows, deep reds, and pink puffs with some berry stick things and the cutest paper pumpkin. Oh, he's good.

"I hope we're not too early. I was worried about hitting traffic, so I rushed her a little bit," he explains nervously.

"You did good, Ben. Don't you worry." I take the flowers from him, and they follow me into the kitchen, where Henry is cutting up some tomatoes and cucumbers for the salad.

He sees Ben and wipes his hand on the dish towel next to him.

"Ben, great to see you again." Henry extends his hand for a welcome shake.

"It smells incredible in here. I could eat a horse," Natalie exclaims and rubs her bowling ball–sized belly. She opens the double oven in the wall beside the fridge. "Where's the turkey, Jones?" She slaps her hand over her mouth and giggles. "Just kidding," she sings.

She stands in front of the open fridge now and begins to rummage for food. "Seriously, what's for dinner? I'm starving. I'm not pregnant with a baby. I think I have a teenage stoner always looking for snacks growing inside of me," she says as she shoves a piece of sliced ham in her mouth.

"Where are those babies? Auntie Nat wants to make them hyper before you put them to bed." Natalie rubs her hands together like she's preparing something evil.

"Um, Nat, need I remind you that you, too, will have a baby soon that others will plot to make hyper."

"Point taken. Well, I'll just play normal with them then." She gives me a look like I just took her ice cream cone away from her.

"Izabel, could you tell me where the washroom is?" Ben asks. "I'd like to wash up before you bring the girls down."

"Well, thank you, Ben, for displaying the proper way to handle children." I look at Natalie to show my approval for Ben's consideration.

"I don't feign knowing anything about babies. I deal with know-it-all teenagers all day."

"See, Jones, he doesn't feign." Natalie pets Ben's back.

I roll my eyes at her again. "Let me show you where the powder room is, Ben." I usher him out of the kitchen.

When I come back to the kitchen, Natalie is shoving more ham in her mouth. She's so impatient.

"I like your Mr. Hardy very much, Natalie, and he definitely knows how to deal with you, in the best way possible, of course." My praise for him doesn't go unnoticed by Natalie, and she begins to blush.

"Yeah, he's a bit all right, I guess."

"Natalie Spencer. You love him, don't you?" Henry begins to tease her.

"You don't know what you're talking about, Henry," she argues but won't look at him.

Henry pokes at her and starts singing, "Nattie and Benny sitting in a tree, K-I-S-S-I-N-G."

Benjamin catches Henry in the act and Natalie shoots him a smug look. "Ha-ha, real mature," she says.

"Oh, hey, Ben, why don't we grab a whiskey?"

I think that was Henry's attempt to remedy the childish outburst he was just caught in.

"Let me tell you about Natalie's twenty-fifth birth-day party."

"Just try it, Rudolph," she retorts.

Henry throws his arm around Benjamin's shoulder in a brotherly way, and they move to the next room. Natalie and I stand in our own daze, watching the men we love walk away together.

I squeeze her hand. "I'm so happy for you, Nat. You guys will be great parents together."

Natalie's smile indicates she's entranced in a pleasant memory. Her reverie is roused by the sound of the girls' laughter as they race across the tiled floor.

She gets down on her knees to greet them. "Come to Auntie, you little slobber monsters."

She pretends to crawl toward them until they are both climbing her like a tree. Natalie calls out for Benjamin to come join her. The four of them roll around on my floor, the girls taking their liberties to step where they want, lick and bite what pleases them, yet they are received by Nat and Ben lovingly, and they completely succumb to these tiny, little humans who are barking babbling orders to them of what they want to do next. I don't know who's having more fun.

It melts my hearts to see how much joy the girls bring to all of our lives, when not so long ago, life could have been so different.

"Let me get them their gifts before it gets too late. Ben, can you grab them from the car?"

"Sure, sweetie." He gives her a kiss on the cheek before letting himself out.

"Sweetie?" Henry questions.

Natalie doesn't respond. She gives Henry a snarl and flips him the middle finger.

Ben opens the front door and loads one box through and then another.

"Natalie, why are the boxes so big?"

"I'm their fairy godmother, and that means I get to buy them whatever I want."

We put the boxes down to see what the girls will do. They start to tear away at the paper, but Natalie pitches in because their snail's pace is killing her. The girls are too interested with the tape that keeps sticking to their little fingers.

From the big boxes, Natalie hands them each a smaller blue Tiffany box. She avoids eye contact with me, knowing that I'll disapprove of the lavish gifts. They start shaking around the blue boxes with little white ribbons and begin laughing uncontrollably at the sound they're making. I can see the anticipation eating away at Natalie, that the girls have no interest in removing the delicate packaging to see what's inside.

"Oh for heaven's sake—let me do it." She sits cross-legged now and slides the girls across the floor closer to her. Natalie unties each bow and simultaneously lifts the lids.

I gasp at the reveal. "Natalie, they're so beautiful."

The light from the chandelier shimmers off the steel, creating a kaleidoscope of sparkles bouncing off the walls.

She takes them out of the boxes and hands one rattle to Faith and the other to Hope. I squat in front of the girls to get a closer look. I'm able to stop Hope's hand from shaking it around long enough to see there's an inscription: "Because even miracles take time. Love, your fairy godmother."

The girls have no idea what the significance of this gift is. But when they're old enough, I'll tell them everything about that day and that I used to lay them on their daddy, skin to skin, when we were all in the hospital so he'd know they were with him. That I would whisper in his ear to wake up so he could hold them and tell them how much he loves his new baby girls. And I'll tell them that I truly believe that the heat and energy from their little bodies saved his life.

I hadn't realized that Mom had come into the room and was watching the girls open their first gift. She gives Natalie an approving look and wipes the tears from her eyes. Natalie responds with a gracious smile. She's been in our lives for so many years, but since that day, my mom has adopted Natalie as one of her own. Mom witnessed firsthand my best friend's true nature and her imperishable love for me.

Natalie recognizes the sadness in the room and pivots.

"Let's see what else Auntie has in here for you." She proceeds to pull out oversized plush toys and blankets. Fuchsia pink knit beanies with matching sweaters. She stops. "Attention, everyone, the pièce de résistance." She holds up matching one-piece, leopard-print leather overalls. We make eye contact. She's looking for my reaction and catches a glimpse of disapproval on my face.

"Relax, it's vegan," she confirms and shakes the hangers.

I begin to clap, and the girls mime my movement. "Let's say thank you to Auntie for your presents." They wiggle with excitement. I look over, and Faith is climbing up Benjamin's legs, pulling at his pants for leverage. He leans and scoops her up and rewards her with a kiss on the cheek.

Henry regards him with a supportive look. "Fatherhood suits you, man."

"All right, everyone," Mom chimes in. "It's bath time. Henry, can you help me get the girls upstairs?"

"I'll help you, Ms. Jones," Ben offers. Faith has made herself comfortable and nuzzled into his neck. She loves finding new warm bodies to fall asleep on.

Ben follows my mom up the stairs. Natalie watches him walk away. She exudes ease. I've been a shoulder for her to cry on or brush off over the years. Regardless who she was dating, male, female, or nonbinary, she was always adamant that she would never settle down. It wasn't her thing, she said. Her most ridiculous argument ever was: "You wouldn't sign a lifetime contract with your cellular company, would you? So why would you sign a marriage license to be with one person forever?"

I think she's found her forever phone.

□ □ □

After dinner, we all slump back in our chairs. We're filled with lasagna and roast beef and vegetables, and everything else that was on Natalie's wish list of foods she absolutely needed to eat tonight. The boys are already a few whiskeys into the evening. Nat and Ben are spending the night, so Henry has enjoyed fueling him with his favorite amber and getting to know him better.

"Izabel, the food was delicious. Thank you so much for having us."

We erupt in laughter at Ben's gracious compliment. Natalie's cackle is a little too chirpy.

"I'm sorry, Ben. We're not laughing at you." Henry offers apologies on behalf of all of us. "We're just a bunch of assholes that spend too much time together."

"Well, I, for one, appreciate the compliment, Ben." I smile. "These two assholes"—I point at Henry and Natalie—"never thank me for feeding them, so I'll prefer you over them anytime."

"Enough about manners, Jones. What's this big surprise you wanted me to see?" She looks around as if looking for a hint. "Also, I just need to say, if you and Henry are going to sneak off to bang one off in the bathroom again, can you maybe speed it up this time?"

"Natalie!" I scoff, trying to discredit her claim.

Henry leans across the table and the two of them high-five.

I acknowledge Ben as I walk into the sitting room to grab the painting. "See what I have to deal with?

Maybe I won't be outnumbered now."

Natalie watches me slowly unwrap the brown paper like a child on Christmas morning, when they know what's in the box is clothes.

"Now I know where your kids get it from. Rip the paper already." Natalie's impatience makes us all laugh.

I finish removing the paper and taunt her, pretending to show her, then pulling it back.

"Drum roll please," I announce.

"Jones, don't fuck around. I'm pregnant; you don't know what I'm capable of."

"Okay, okay, I present to you *After Eve*." I turn the painting and rest it on the table for a clearer view.

Natalie slaps her hands over her face, presumably astounded. Ben just looks confused.

"Jones, is this what I think it is—and where did you find it?

"Henry found it in New York. He took me there for the night a couple of weeks ago and we bought it."

"Hold on. Back up a bit. This is no yada-yada story." Natalie stands and walks to my side of the table to take a closer look at the painting.

Poor Ben, the moment is lost on him. He's unaware of the significance of the painting.

I begin to tell the story, minus a few unpleasant details, of Henry visiting his parents in New York and about him reading Charlie's journal. "Here, look." I motion for Henry to pass me his phone. I scroll through the photos—oops, not that one—until I get to the photo of Charlie's entry about Eve, and I hand it to Natalie.

She scans through the letter, focusing in and out to make some of the illegible cursive bigger.

Natalie isn't a sentimental gal, but she's visibly moved.

"Well! And then what happened?" she presses.

"Like I said, Henry tracked it down through Sotheby's, and we went to the auction and bid on it. And won." My tone is self-congratulatory.

"It's such a piece of our history, Henry knew we had to have it. Especially because it was the last one he painted of Eve."

Natalie and I admire the painting. She talks about the brushstrokes and the absence of color and the depth. Everything she's good at.

"Who knew you'd have to pay money for an original Charles Rudolph? You're sleeping with the man's grandson—and, well, technically you slept with Charlie too," Natalie jokes.

"Ha-ha, but tell me about it, and it wasn't cheap." I cringe at the amount of money we dropped on this, but it was worth every penny to have a piece of Eve with me forever.

"Ben, can I pour you another whiskey, man? The girls will be wrapped up with this for a while now."

"No thanks," Ben says, seeming preoccupied. "Did you say Charles Rudolph?"

"Yeah, he was my granddad. He was a painter. Well, obviously." Henry points at the painting, affirming his statement.

"Will you excuse me for a minute?" Ben leaves the room.

Natalie calls out after him. "Babe, where are you going?"

A few minutes later, Ben is back with his phone in his hand. He hands it to Henry and shows him a photo.

It's a photo of Charlie's *Forever Eve*. The first painting he did of Eve the month he spent visiting her at the Blue Note.

Henry's face contorts with confusion. "How do you know about his painting?" he asks.

Ben mimes Henry's confusion. "It's hanging in my parents' house in the library study.

Henry tips his glass to his lips and gulps down the last few drops of whiskey, and then looks back at Ben. "Are your parents art collectors?" he inquires.

"Not really art collectors, but this one they had to have. It was special to them. Well, special to my mom really. The lady in the portrait was her great-aunt.

"Her name was Eve. Eve Baker."

21

We're all speechless as we try to process the information we just heard. A slew of emotions come flooding back. Images of Eve begin to flash before me. Pearls cascading down her back, Josephine's soft lips, the way Charlie would look through her eyes into her soul, professing his unspoken love to her. I've spent years pining to find out what happened to Eve, if she moved on, if she ever found love again. My heart bleeds for her again at this moment. I'm severed. Do I keep her a mystery, or does her memory die with me right here, right now?

The room remains silent, except the apprehension of who will speak up first is deafening.

The four of us stand together, mesmerized by a painting of a woman's history that has singularly touched each of our lives so profoundly, directly and indirectly.

Natalie cracks first. "Benjamin, please tell us what the fuck *you're* talking about."

"Natalie," Ben projects with paralleled attitude, "I think it's you three who need to tell me what the fuck you're talking about."

Good on Ben. I'm totally loving this guy more and more. His sweet face and demeanor deceive me. I laugh under my breath. I still can't say anything. I understand all the words that came out of his mouth, but I'm in such a bewildered state I can't even begin to understand what Ben has just disclosed to us.

Henry pipes in. "Ben, so what you're saying is Eve was your great-aunt on your . . ."

"On my mother's side."

Natalie, Henry, and I remain muted again. I know we're all trying to conjure a way to tell this man that his great aunt was a dancer and much more at a brothel.

"You see, Ben, Charles Rudolph, the man who did these two paintings and many more in his lifetime, was my grandfather." Henry stops. I can see that he's trying to choose his words delicately. "And Eve, your great-aunt, was his . . ." Henry looks at me for guidance.

"His muse?" I offer.

"Oh for Pete's sake, you two. Just rip the Band-Aid off. Ben's a big boy. Charlie and Eve were lovers. They met in a whorehouse, had a love affair, and then Charlie left her to marry some socialite." Natalie peers at us and mouths the word *pussies*.

"I think I'll take that drink now, Henry," Ben appeals.

Henry pours two two-finger pours and hands a lowball to Ben. The clink of their glasses is followed by a much-needed gulp of the amber liquid.

"Why don't we all sit down? There is so much more context to this story that you should probably know, Ben."

I usher everyone into the living room in hopes of providing a more comfortable environment for Ben. What is the level of comfort needed, however, for someone who's just learned a loved one was a prostitute?

Respectively, we pick our seats and settle in for the unveiling that's about to ensue.

"Ben," Henry begins, "why don't you start by telling us about Eve? I think that might be helpful to bring some perspective to what's going on here."

Ben looks pensive. "Well, I didn't know her at all. She died very young, during childbirth, I was told, but she and my grandmother were very close, and I know she was devastated by her death for years."

My heart aches as the pieces of Eve start to break away in my mind. I feel like I'm imploding from the inside, finally learning how it all ended for her.

Ben continues, "The family didn't talk much about her, other than there was a bit of a scandal about her getting pregnant late in life, like late thirties, I think. There was never any mention or discussion of who the father was." Ben leans forward and takes his wallet from his back pocket. He pulls out a photo and hands it to me.

"I don't know why I carry this around with me," he explains. "I always just felt like I needed her with me, even though I'd never met her. This was the only photo my mom ever had of her. I remember being a kid and staring at it for hours, wondering who she was and what she was like when she was young. There's something about her eyes in this photo—like she is looking at me, wanting to tell me her story."

In my hands I hold a black-and-white photo of Eve. Her beautiful dark hair is flowing down her back; she's wearing a long silk gown; her shoulders are covered with a fur stole; and a string of pearls tied in a loose knot rests just below her breasts.

I drop the photo and begin to cry. From what? Happiness, sorrow, from the embarrassment that I yearn to go back and experience the passion and energy that I felt every time Charlie touched her?

The air in the room is heavy. I look to see Henry's reaction at the new revelation. He's counting his fingers, doing some mental math. I know I'm thinking what he's thinking.

"Are you okay, Izabel?" Ben asks with concern in his voice.

I wipe away the tears with my sleeve and hand the photo to Natalie. She's about to say something, but Henry interjects.

"Ben, there's something you need to know about your ... about Eve. Charlie and Eve met in Detroit. They were both very young, just barely adults. I spent a lot of time with my grandfather when I was young. He was very ill, bedridden most of the time, and we would talk for hours about his life's adventures. My grandfather came from a wealthy family but was on a quest and desperate to find his own path. He had the means to travel to different cities and countries without much disapproval from his family in the beginning. One day he told me a story about a woman he had fallen deeply and madly in love with, but that he could never have because of the life she was living."

Ben listens attentively, following Henry's recount, but he seems unfazed by the story so far.

Natalie's face lights up. She blurts out, "Oh my god, you guys could be related?" She points at Henry.

Ben perks up. "I don't understand what you are trying to tell me."

Henry continues, "How do I say this respectfully? Eve was a dancer at a gentleman's club, and that's where she and Charlie met. They were intimate with each other, as well."

Ben scratches at the scruff on his chin and then lets out a sigh. "And how do the paintings fit into all of this?" he asks.

"The paintings are a product of their time spent together. He also kept a journal about her for years, professing his love for her and his regrets about leaving her," Henry qualifies, as if he's apologizing for Charlie's choices.

Ben gets up and paces the room, absorbing the information he's just received. He pours himself another drink. "Are you saying that Charlie was the father to Eve's child?"

Henry scratches at the day's growth of scruff on his face. "No, it's not possible. The timing doesn't add up. She continued working at the club well after Charlie had already moved back to New York and married my grandmother. From what he wrote in his journal, he essentially stalked her a few times after that, but there was never any mention about them being together again."

I watch Henry swirl at the notion that nothing is impossible. Just because Charlie didn't tell him doesn't mean it didn't happen.

Natalie has moved herself into my chair and is practically sitting on top of me. We watch our loves pace around the room together, each processing this new information on their own.

She whispers in my ear. "I can't believe what's happening right now. Wish we had some popcorn."

I shush her. I'm not sure what emotions I'm feeling right now. This revelation is tugging at my heart. I've spent so many years thinking about Eve. She lost her life to her love child, but who was the father? I want to tell Ben about my past life regression experience and about how intimately I know Eve, but this is too much for all of us right now. I can't throw this into the mix. I'm not sure I'm ready to share that part of my life with him yet either.

"Ben, I know this is a lot to take in, for all of us, actually. We're all basing this on assumptions right now. I'm sure this is a very big coincidence."

I'm not sure who Henry's trying harder to convince, Ben or himself.

Ben and Henry stand face-to-face now. Ben studies Henry, as if trying to penetrate his cerebral cortex for clues.

He extends his hand to Henry. He accepts it, and they pull in for a dude hug and pat each other on the back a few times.

"I just think this is all so cool. I don't know if it's all the booze or because I already consider you and Izabel family, but this really is great."

Natalie and I let out a loud exhale. I was becoming light-headed from the tension that was building.

She hops off my lap and wraps her arms around Ben.

"Wow—that was some heavy shit, sweetie. I can't believe how calm you're being." Natalie plants a kiss on his cheek.

"Who doesn't love a good scandal? So, if there is more to this story, then that's a bonus, isn't it?" Ben shrugs.

"How amazing is my boyfriend?" Natalie showcases him to us like a prize on a game show. "Now, if you'll excuse us, I'm going to bang my boyfriend and christen my bedroom, because my pregnancy hormones are on overdrive."

She begins to drag Ben from the room, but he stops her in her tracks. Then he turns to Henry and me.

"Honestly," he says, "I want to thank you both for everything tonight. I'm privileged to be part of this friendship you all have. I've never experienced anything like this before." We exchange earnest smiles.

Natalie clutches her shirt over her heart. "You're getting extra special loving now. Let's go before I strip you down right here, right now," she orders.

"Yes, boss." The two of them rush out of the room before we can say goodnight.

Henry and I flop down on the couch next to each other.

"Well, that was an unexpected turn of events," he says, sinking deeper into the sofa. "I honestly don't know how to feel about all of this. I'm kind of on edge right now. The magnitude of this ongoing mystery is spectacularly overwhelming. I thought I knew Eve and Charlie's entire history. But, I guess this is where the story ends."

I snuggle in close to comfort him. He kisses the top of my head, and then kisses the side of my face. He gently tugs at my chin so my lips meet his. I feel him exhale, releasing all the air from his lungs. We unleash ravaging kisses on each other. We're grasping at these emotions, and carnal desire overcomes us.

He lifts his shirt over his head, exposing his muscular torso. I drag my tongue and teeth down his chest and bite and nibble at his skin. He stands, and I fumble to undo his belt. I unzip him free, and his pants and boxers fall to the ground. I can't devour him fast enough. The buildup of our discovery tonight is pulling at us to the core on a cellular level. We won't be satisfied until we feast on each other. He fills my mouth with his raging readiness. I hear the hissing sound of pleasure escape from between his teeth. He wraps his fingers through my hair, and I take him deeper in, over and over, until he pulls away and lays me on the ground. Then he rips at my tights wildly. He can't get to me fast enough.

"I need you inside me, Henry!" I cry. His fingers are deep in me now, finding my sweet spot with every push. Henry replaces his fingers with his swollen cock. He slides his fingers in my mouth. Then he leans down closer to my ear, and with a breathy command, he tells me to taste my pleasure. I release a glorious moan, and like a wild stag, he bucks into me unrelentingly. We make love for hours with so much passion, as if we're uncovering secrets within each other until we are shattering around each other. He collapses on top of me, physically and emotionally drained.

"I love you so much, Izabel. You've been my entire

existence, even before you and I existed. You are my then, my now, and my forever." He releases a fulfilled sigh.

I bestow little kisses on the scars on his chest—our constant reminder of our mortality.

"You're stuck with me now, Mr. Rudolph." I chuckle.

"I wouldn't have it any other way, Dr. Jones." He kisses me tenderly.

I nestle in under his arm and lie on his chest. His breathing is deep. I know he's still struggling to understand what happened with Charlie and Eve, even after our attempted salacious exorcism. I twirl at his graying chest hairs, contemplating if I should bring it up again.

"You know it's not entirely impossible that Charlie was the father of Eve's baby. I mean, we know he saw her at least once after he left. Maybe they had a secret affair, years later. Aren't you the least bit curious?" I ask, trying to avoid sounding insistent.

Henry strokes my hair. "I don't know, Iz. It's Charlie's history. Maybe it's not our business to know. There's a reason he didn't disclose this to anyone. Maybe it's just better to let sleeping dogs lie."

"Yeah, I guess. It just doesn't feel like it's over. Maybe we owe it to her to wake the proverbial dog and find out the truth." Secretly, I hope my projecting will pique his interest in pursuing this.

Henry threads his fingers through mine and traces a heart in the palm of my hand.

"All right," he surrenders.

I sit straight up. "What? Are you serious? You want to know what happened?" I squeal a little too loudly.

Realizing I'm sitting here naked, I peek around to make sure nobody's come downstairs. "You really want to do this—find out if it was Charlie's baby?"

"Yeah, I really do." Henry smiles and pulls me into his embrace.

And there, in the middle of our dining room, we sit naked in the dark, except for a stream of moonlight that shines perfectly on his face. We plan our next step into our history, after Eve.

Acknowledgments

To my husband and kids, thank you for the constant love and encouragement to keep going on this crazy ride.

To my amazing team at Hadleigh House Publishing. Thank you for trusting that I'm still making good choices, your support means so much to me.

To my Nikki, you've been in my corner from day one. Thank you for bossing me around.

To all of my other people, you know who you are and you know how grateful I am to have you in my life.

And last but definitely not least, thank you to my readers and followers. You all have this incredible sense of when I might be doubting myself and you send the kindest words when I least expect it and need it the most. You give me all the feels!

About JB Lexington

JB Lexington is the best-selling author of *Forever Eve*, a steamy romance that explores past life regression, friendships, and self-discovery.

When she's not writing sexy stories after dark at her kitchen table, she runs a successful construction company that she co-owns with her husband.

The beautiful city of Toronto is where she calls home with her family and two dogs. With her nutrition background and vegetarian diet, you can always find JB in the kitchen, with a full glass of pinot grigio, creating new tasty dishes to share.

JB Lexington's dream is to get a drag queen make-over and she is on a constant quest to find the perfect pillow.

www.jblexington.com

Manufactured by Amazon.ca
Bolton, ON